Anaconda's Treasure
The Hearst Free Library

Marian Geil

Copyright, 1998, by The Hearst Free Library, Anaconda, Montana
All rights reserved.

No part of this book may be reproduced, in any form, without written permission except in the case of brief quotations embodied in critical articles or reviews. For information, address The Hearst Free Library, 401 Main Street, Anaconda, MT 59711

10 09 08 07 06 05 04 03 02 01 00 99   10 9 8 7 6 5 4 3 2 1

Cover painting by Paul A. Hawkins
Designed and typeset in Minion by Geoffrey Wyatt, Helena, Montana
Printed by BookCrafters, Chelsea, Michigan

Publisher's Cataloging-in-Publication
(Provided by Quality Books, Inc)

Geil, Marian.
    Anaconda's Treasure: the Hearst Free Library / Marian Geil. – 1st ed.
    p. cm.
    Includes bibliographical references and index.
    ISBN 0-9664922-0-X

    1. Hearst Free Library (Anaconda, Mont.) 2. Anaconda (Mont.)—History. 3. Public Libraries—Montana—Anaconda. I. Title.

Z733.H43G45 1998   027.4'786'87
                                    QBI98-779

To all the generations of Anaconda readers who have loved, appreciated and supported the Hearst Free Library, this book is dedicated.

Marian Geil

Anaconda's Treasure: The Hearst Free Library
Table of Contents

Preface iv

Chapter 1
How It All Came About: The Big Four 1

Chapter 2
The Hearst Lake Story. 9

Chapter 3
Phoebe 15

Chapter 4
Phoebe Apperson Hearst Library, Lead, South Dakota 21

Chapter 5
The Temporary Library. 25

Chapter 6
Building and Dedication of New Library 33

Chapter 7
Library Turned Over to City, 1903 43

Chapter 8
The Board of Trustees and Its Illustrious First Chairman . . . 49

Chapter 9
Some Other Board Members of Note 57

Chapter 10
Hitting the Highlights in Library Board Minutes 67

Chapter 11
Treasures Within the Library 77

Chapter 12
The Librarians 95

Chapter 13
The Custodians 111

Chapter 14
Reminiscences and Snappy Research Questions 117

Chapter 15
The 'Potent Factor' 123

Bibliography. 129

Acknowledgments 131

Index 133

Preface

In the mountains of Southwestern Montana lies a modern day ghost town—a ghost in the common meaning of that term applied to so many western towns whose mines have played out, and the townspeople have moved on to newer strikes, or more lucrative locations. Always a 'one-horse town,' Anaconda, Montana's sole reason for existence was the Anaconda Company's copper smelter which processed the ore from the 'richest hill on earth' at Butte, 25 miles to the east. When the copper smelter closed in 1980, that sole reason for existence was gone—and as should be expected, a fair number of the population packed up and left, too. But the roots of many were deep in the little town, as deep as the tunnels of the Anaconda mine in the Butte hill which gave the town its name; and 15 years after the smelter closed down forever, the community still clings tenaciously to life.

The town is off the interstate highway several miles, and visitors who are attracted by the scenic by-ways of this beautiful state are lured off I-90 by the 'Pintler Scenic Route' designation. If they don't drive straight through town on Commercial street, which is one-way going west, or Park street, which is one-way going east, they occasionally find themselves going south on Main street, where they find a mural proclaiming 'Anaconda, where Main street meets the mountains,' and it does, literally. At the northern termination of Main street is the picturesque little building which was the passenger depot of the Butte-Anaconda and Pacific Railway, once recognized as the shortest incorporated railroad in the world. Behind the depot rise the foothills that were occupied by the original smelter, long gone, the ruins of which are commonly referred to as the 'Old Works.' The southern end of Main street is graced by the Deer Lodge county court house, a handsome structure designed by architect Charles Bell, and now on the National Register of Historic Places, behind which rise the foothills of the Anaconda Range. The town nestles in a little valley between these mountains, giving the inhabitants, according to this writer's pioneer grandmother, the feeling of being in the bottom of a teacup.

Urban Renewal and some basic spectacular fires have removed a good number of the impressive business blocks of Anaconda, but as those occasional tourists proceed up Main, they pass the old Daly Bank building, lately occupied by a pool hall, and the two remaining stories of the famous Montana Hotel, which has been partially demolished to the point where it is unrecognizable from its original grandeur. They pass the fine little post office and the art nouveau Washoe Theater, both on the National Register of Historic Places; and find themselves confronted at the Fourth Street intersection by a classic gem of architectural beauty on a green oasis of lawn, midway up to the court house. They stop, climb the graceful granite steps which lead to a pillared portico, and look at the arched marble "Hearst Free Library" sign over the massive oak doorway.

A library! This is the place to get some information! As they enter, the librarian looks up, recognizes the shorts, flowered shirt, sneakers, large purse over the shoulder, camera around the neck, and anticipates the first question. " What is that mountain of black stuff we passed on our way into town?"

"That's the slag pile," she explains. "That's the residue left from the processing of the copper ore at the smelter, which is no longer in existence." "Where's the mine?" is usually the next question. She explains that the mines are in Butte, 25 miles away, and that Anaconda was a smelter town. "Oh, a copper smelter," the tourist says. "Would that be the Kennecott company?" "No," the librarian smiles patiently. "You are in Anaconda, Montana, home of the Anaconda Company, once one of the world's major copper producers." Sometimes the tourist recognizes his gaffe, and changes the subject.

"This is a lovely building, what was it before it was a library?" The librarian explains that the library was constructed in 1898 for that purpose, by Phoebe Apperson Hearst, whose husband George was a business partner of Marcus Daly, the founder of the town. "Any relation to William Randolph Hearst? We've been to San Simeon."

If the tourists and the librarian had more time, the story of how the library, and perhaps the town itself, were the result of a chance meeting in the gold fields of Utah over 100 years ago, would make fine telling.

1995 marked the 100th anniversary, of the Hearst Free Library in Anaconda, and 1998 the centennial observance of this attractive building. What better reason is needed for the telling of the story?

1 How It All Came About: The Big Four

A memorable diorama, formerly at the State Historical Society in Helena, and now located at the World Museum of Mining in Butte, depicts Marcus Daly, one of Montana's famous 'copper kings,' giving his sales pitch on the Anaconda mine, to his potential business partners from San Francisco, George Hearst and James B. Haggin. If Hearst and Haggin and the third man involved, Lloyd Tevis, had not come through with financial backing for Daly on his copper venture, the history of Anaconda, the town, would probably have been considerably different, or at least, considerably delayed in beginning. For one thing, Anaconda would not have had its fine public library, which is a direct result of Marcus Daly's acquaintance with George Hearst.

Hearst and Daly had much in common, both coming from humble rural backgrounds. Daly, as a young man, worked his way from Ireland to New York, and thence to the gold fields of California. Hearst left a farm in Missouri, following the same gleam of wealth to be found in the far west. But of all the hundreds of eager young men who answered the call of gold, these two both had an unusual sense for finding the real paydirt. And, possibly more important, they understood how to get the financial backing necessary to develop the most promising discoveries.

George Hearst, as a boy on that Missouri farm, used to drive hogs to the nearby lead mines for sale. He developed a great interest in mining, reading all the books available to him on the subject. The miners took an interest in the eager youth, and took him into the mines to answer his questions. So even with little formal schooling, he gained, early in life, a technical knowledge to add to his almost uncanny instinct about finding minerals. As early as age 15 he was gleaning bits of galena that made him 'four to six bits' a day from the Virginia mine near St. Clair, about a

George Hearst

Lloyd Tevis

mile from his home. The owners of the smelters were French and had nice homes with fine furnishings. They took a shine to George and tried to teach him to speak French. He credited them with having taught him about the lead mines, and also copper and iron. George said that farming was such a slow way to make a living, and even then he could see that mining was the way to make money.

His father died when George was in his early twenties, leaving him to care for his mother, sister and crippled brother. He bought rights to his father's estate after his mother remarried four years later, and went to work in a general store owned by a friend. Soon he was able to buy his own general store at Judith Springs, which was a busy place at a trading crossroads. It was here he learned about the California gold rush. He talked over going to California with his mother and she was not keen on it until he pointed out that people were making $40 or $50 a day there; and she believed George was knowledgeable enough to do that too. He sold his father's interest in some copper mines and other mining interests for $1900, and made a trusted family friend his agent to handle his affairs while he was to be away on a journey he expected to last for two years. He set off in May 1850 with a party of fifteen, including several cousins.

It was a difficult journey. He contracted cholera and was so ill in

How It All Came About: The Big Four

Wyoming, he was sure he was going to die, but he trudged on, and finally made it to the colorful camps of Placerville, Jackass Gulch and El Dorado.

The road to prosperity was not an easy one, even in the midst of the gold rush days in California. For ten years George worked hard, with pick and shovel; buying, trading, rediscovering properties that had been cast aside, until he had accumulated a fairly handsome stake. The Ophir mine was the first claim recorded on the famous Comstock Lode, which was in the region on the California-Nevada border known by its Indian named, Wasseau, soon simplified to Washoe. George purchased an interest in that mine from its discoverer, William Thomas Page Comstock, when he realized that the 'heavy black stuff' which was a pain to the gold prospectors, was silver ore. He built a smelter to process the ore, and by 1860, had realized a good profit from the venture.

In 1860, however, upon hearing of the serious illness of his widowed mother, George sold a partial interest in the Ophir and returned to Missouri, where he paid off the debts of the family farm, and stayed with his mother until her death.

One of the frequent visitors to his ailing mother was a second cousin, Phoebe Elizabeth Apperson, who had been just a child when George left for the gold fields. She had grown into an

James B. Haggin

Marcus Daly

enthusiastic and attractive young school teacher, and she found the miner from California to be very interesting company. He courted Phoebe, much to the delight of his mother, for Phoebe's middle name, Elizabeth, had been bestowed in her honor; but the Appersons felt George at 42 was much too old for their 18 year old daughter, and did all they could to discourage the match. Phoebe was a determined young lady, however, and when George returned to California, his young bride accompanied him, planning to be a miner's wife and live with him in the gold camps. They established their home in San Francisco.

A few years later, feeling the Comstock was finally playing out, George went a little farther afield to the Park City, Utah area, and prospected a claim there he had heard about. He was not impressed with it, but while there he ran into Marcus Daly, who had been inspecting "a little hole in the ground" for his employers, the Walker Brothers of Salt Lake. They were not interested, it turned out, but Daly felt it had potential, and suggested George should take a look at it.

George found "the little hole" of great interest indeed, and called upon his acquaintances, James B. Haggin and Lloyd Tevis of San Francisco for financial backing. Being well aware of Hearst's astuteness for finding a good property, Haggin and Tevis joined with Hearst in what was to become a major power in the history of American mining. By 1883, the little hole which had become the Ontario mine, had poured out $17 million in silver for the Hearst-Haggin-Tevis syndicate.

Marcus Daly, roving prospector for the Walker Brothers, while superintendent for them at the Ophir mine south of Salt Lake, had met and married his wife, Maggie Evans, in 1872. George Hearst was a guest at the wedding, and appropriately enough, gave the happy couple a gift of silver. The friendship of the two men was firm and lifelong. Perhaps George could feel an affinity for Daly in this marriage too, as Marcus was 31 and Maggie only 18.

George's interests turned to South Dakota in 1877 when he got a tip that there was a good gold prospect there. With the Indian troubles and all at the time, Dakota was a pretty wild place, but George finally ended up putting up the money for the prospect himself, and was soon joined by Haggin and Tevis. The

Homestake mine produced the second fortune for the trio.

By the time Marcus Daly had prospected the Butte hill for the Walker Brothers, and could not interest them in what he felt to be a very promising lead in copper, he immediately approached Hearst, Haggin and Tevis, and Anaconda came into being with the Washoe Copper Mining Company a successor to Hearst's first mining corporation, the Washoe Gold and Silver Company from the old Comstock days. The trio had become a quartet, or as they were known in mining circles, the Big Four.

The search for a site for the copper smelter to handle the ore from Daly's Anaconda mine has been well documented elsewhere, with sites on the Big Hole and the Madison river, as well as the one on Warm Springs creek being considered. The Anaconda reduction works on Warm Springs creek were constructed in 1883, and the town of Anaconda was platted.

In an autobiography written in 1890, Hearst mentions that in the town of Anaconda, Daly had a fine hotel. Urban legend has it that when Marcus Daly was building his magnificent hotel, with the idea that one day it might house the legislators when Anaconda became state capital, he was showing it off proudly to George Hearst, who suggested that the three story hotel looked squatty. Marcus supposedly hailed his building contractor and instructed him to "Put on another story so it won't look so damn squat." In the *Anaconda Review*, Anaconda's first newspaper, the building was referred to when it was almost finished as 'The Hearst Hotel.' By the time it was opened with its grand ball in July 1888, however, it had become 'The Montana.'

No kindly historian has recorded for us the reason that the mountain lake at the foot of 'Old Baldy' southwest of Anaconda became Hearst Lake, but isn't it easy to imagine these robust pioneer miners grouped around the makeshift bar of O'Shaughnnesy's tent saloon in the fledgling city, toasting their new partnership and shaking the dice; "Winner of the first shake gets the mountain, winner of the second shake gets the lake!" The Hearst Lake story will be related in a separate chapter.

George Hearst did not spend much time in Montana, Lloyd Tevis even less. Hearst was elected to the United States Senate from California in 1886, after serving in the state legislature, and spent most of the last years of his life in Washington, D.C. He died there on February 28, 1891.

Lloyd Tevis, the fourth and not so well known (at least in Anaconda) member of the Big Four, was a brother-in-law and life-long associate of J. B. Haggin. They had vast land holdings in California. He was a dry goods merchant, a miner, a real estate broker, a banker; but above all, according to the *Anaconda Standard* of July 30, 1899, he was a financier. When the Great Fire in St. Louis, Missouri, wiped out the insurance firm for which Tevis was working in 1849, he determined to start afresh and headed for the gold fields of California. He toiled for nine months with pick and shovel in the diggings of El Dorado, with no success. He moved on to Sacramento and took a job in the recorder's office, which position gave him great insight into land values. He started speculating on a small scale, and was very successful. In 1850 he went into partnership with a friend from his youth in Kentucky, James B. Haggin, in the practice of law; but during the next 50 years, the law practice became lost as the firm became one of the most prestigious ever known in the world of business and finance.

Tevis was more of a patient accumulator than a bold investor. He and Haggin were among the largest land owners of the world and were prominent in commercial and industrial affairs of which the interest in the smelter in Anaconda was but a small part. Tevis was connected with nearly every commercial enterprise in California in his lifetime; California Steam Navigation, the state telegraph company, for which he conducted negotiations for the purchase by Western Union; he was president of the Southern Pacific Railroad, and of the Pacific Ice Company. The California dry dock and the California Market were his projects. He started the Pacific Express Company which was bought by Wells Fargo and Company, and he became president of that great corporation. He owned mines in California, Nevada, Utah and Idaho, 1300 miles of stage lines; his cattle and sheep were numbered by the tens of thousands, and his land properties by the square mile.

Mr. Tevis has no monuments in Montana, but he obviously played his part in the development of our area with the quiet capability that marked his life as an extremely successful business man.

And how about the man for whom Mt. Haggin is named? James Ben Ali Haggin was born in Kentucky, where his forebears settled in 1774. His father was a lawyer, his mother was the daughter of a Christian Turk with the surname Ben Ali. Haggin studied the law in his father's office. As with all the rest of the partners in this adventure, the discovery of gold in California drew Haggin from a successful law practice in New Orleans to Sacramento, where he became a deputy clerk of the California Supreme Court. It was while in this position that he renewed acquaintance with his old friend from Kentucky, Lloyd Tevis, and they opened their law office, which was so successful, they moved to San Francisco.

These two men complemented each other perfectly. Haggin, quiet and imperturbable; Tevis, talkative and ubiquitous, they both were endowed with the necessary vision and ambition to take part in the momentous activities that were going on around them. They loaned money. They financed express, railroad and telegraph enterprises. They invested in land. When they formed the mining syndicate with George Hearst in 1870, Haggin was the dominant personality. He developed the properties from the prospect state, and watched the expenditures. Tevis handled the finances, and Hearst, with his amazing knowledge of ores, found the mines. Haggin had an unwavering loyalty for both Hearst and Daly. When Marcus came on board to turn the syndicate into the Big Four of the mining world, his part was to concentrate on the development of the Reduction Works for their copper venture. At one point Tevis became apprehensive about the amount of money Daly was pouring into the property, but after Haggin came to Butte and looked things over, he expressed his support of the way things were progressing, and the work went ahead. Very likely much of Tevis' apprehension came when the Old Works burned at Anaconda, and Haggin wired Marcus Daly permission to undertake the rebuilding of the works with all possible speed.

Aside from their mutual interest in mining, Hearst, Haggin and Daly shared another less remunerative activity, an enthusiasm for horse racing. Hearst owned tracks and horses in California, but with him it was not the serious pastime it became with Daly and Haggin. Daly, of course, had his tracks in Butte and Anaconda, and his world famous breeding farm in the

Bitterroot valley. Haggin began breeding horses in 1881 in California on a modest scale, but eventually returned to Kentucky where he bought the Elmdorf breeding farm, and by 1912 he held 10,000 acres and was the largest individual land owner in the state. It was claimed that he owned 3 times as many thoroughbreds as any other man. Ben Ali, winner of the Kentucky Derby in 1886 was a Haggin horse.

At the time Haggin finally gave up horse breeding, he stated, "A man can't afford to be bossed by his pleasures—that is worse than being bossed by your business." Upon horse breeding as a business, he went on to say, "It is a fascinating occupation, and there is a lot of sentiment in it—more than in copper mines and railways; but if you go in for horses, you will find you cannot do much else properly; and I have not enjoyed serving two masters. It is a dangerous occupation too, for it fosters the worst habit of the American people. I mean the habit of gambling, which begins in the majority of cases in race track tips." So he gave up horse breeding and turned the Kentucky estate into a tobacco farm, which raised 500,000 pounds of tobacco a year; certainly little realizing at the time that tobacco was another bad habit for the American people, the consequences of which were not to be suspected for almost a hundred years.

After the Anaconda company ceased to be a partnership and was turned into the Amalgamated Copper Company in 1899, Haggin's infrequent visits to Montana ceased, and he spent most of his later years in New York City. With Marcus Daly's death in 1900, Haggin became the last survivor of this dynamic group, and he was one of Daly's sincerest mourners.

Sources for this chapter were:

Robinson, Judith; *The Hearsts: An American Dynasty.* U. of Delaware Press, 1991.

Shoebotham, H. Minar; *Anaconda: Life of Marcus Daly, the Copper King.* Stackpole Co., Pa. 1956.

Fielder, Mildred; *Treasure of Homestake Gold.* North Plains Pr. So. Dakota, 1970.

Marcosson, Isaac F. *Anaconda.* Dodd, Mead; New York, 1956.

Anaconda Standard, Sept. 13, 1914.

2 The Hearst Lake Story

he building of the dam at Hearst Lake to provide the necessary water for the smelting works and community is an interesting story in itself. On October 14, 1897, plans were finalized by the Anaconda Copper Mining Company to utilize the waters of Hearst Gulch for a fine new water system capable of serving a city of 50,000. The company had acquired and located rights to all the water in the gulch, including Lake Hearst, a crescent shaped mountain lake about 3/4 mile in length by 1/4 mile in width, which nestles at the foot of Mt. Haggin at an elevation of 8,200 feet, or 2900 feet above the level of the street in front of the Montana Hotel.(The U.S. Geological Survey marker at the front step of the hotel was always a popular reference point.)

By the first of November there were over 100 men at work at the lake; masons, carpenters and laborers, and a large number of teams building the embankment for raising the lake surface and putting the outlet pipes into place. The plans consisted of raising the banks of the lake about 20 feet, which would increase its storage capacity to over 750,000,000 gallons. This, with the other waters in the gulch, would provide a daily flow of fully 400,000,000 in addition to the volume of over 1,000,000 at the time flowing into the existing reservoir from the old source of supply.

A six mile long steel pipeline was constructed to convey the waters of the lake to an entirely new reservoir in the same gulch where the existing reservoir was located. The new reservoir was 70 feet higher than the old one, and when filled, was 320 feet higher than the survey marker in front of the hotel. The new reservoir was formed by building an earth and masonry dam across a narrow place in the gulch, and made a pond 1300 feet long and 400 feet wide, and 60 feet deep at the deepest part.

In order to insure the utmost purity and supply the best water possible, and incidentally to add to the beauty of the spot, the supply main from Lake Hearst was planned to terminate in a fountain in the center of the reservoir where it was expected, according to a news item in the *Anaconda Standard*, that a solid jet of water 2 or 3 inches in diameter would be thrown from the central orifice fully 200 feet vertically into the air, while around the base of the fountain would be a fringe of spray consisting of rows of jets rising to various heights and at various angles. The newspaper trumpeted that the fountain would undoubtedly be the largest in the world.

All the valves regulating the flow from each reservoir were planned to be electrically controlled and capable of operation from the office of the water department, thus enabling the superintendent to have complete control.

A fine wagon road was built to Lake Hearst at very great expense, running through a pretty pine forest and with splendid views of the valleys of Warm Springs creek and the Deer Lodge river. Citizens of Anaconda were invited to visit the works at Lake Hearst and the reservoir, as the roads were good and it was a pleasant drive. The engineers and assistants were instructed to explain the works to visitors.

By December 20, however, the picture was not quite so rosy, when 43 men at work at the lake went on strike, in protest of the company raising the price of their board to $1.00 per day. The company explained that before December 1, when the roads were good and there was no snow to impede the progress of hauling provisions to the lake, it was possible to feed the crew for seventy five cents each. But the arrival of winter's snow made the road much more difficult and the board was raised to $1.00. Wages for the men were $2.50 per day. The strikers were informed that if they were not back on the job by noon, they would be replaced. They chose to come to town; the company sent 50 other men out to take their places, and work resumed as usual.

The original plans stated that if an accident should happen to the supply pipe leading from Lake Hearst to the reservoir, the capacity of the 2 reservoirs would be ample at all times to supply the city until repairs were made.

The "accident," when it finally happened, was not to the

pipeline coming from the lake, but to the reservoir itself; an unusually wet spring in 1938 left the reservoirs particularly full, and on the evening of July 27, the dam at the upper reservoir gave way, leaving a gaping V shaped hole in the bank. The wall of water washed out the lower dam and spread on down the valley, inundating much of the Anaconda business district under three feet of water.

Ole Larson, caretaker at the dam, was able to summon aid

July 27, 1938; 6:30 p.m. Water flows from Reservoir Gulch.

Corner of Park and Main. It took an hour to reach this point.

August 1994. Remains of the Battery House.

August 1994. Part of the dam at Hearst Lake.

from farmers and peace officers to warn residents of the approaching water. Sections of the city from Fourth street to Warm Springs creek were inundated, the major damage being to businesses with flooded basements in the downtown area. City Engineer Charles Nicely estimated the water was 4 feet deep at Cedar street and Park avenue, which is the lowest section of the city. Damage was reported as far away as the game farm at Warm Springs, where the creek, which was out of its banks at that point, drowned or liberated several hundred pheasants when their pens were washed away.

McMonigle's ranch was located at the mouth of the gulch where the reservoirs were. One of their barns was washed off its foundation and a stallion was reported as a casualty. The water swirled around the ranch home, but the family escaped without injury.

The breaking of the dam did not curtail the city water supply, as water was supplied from other sources. The waters from Hearst Lake were allowed to run into Warm Springs creek in their natural manner until 1967, when the Butte Water Company rebuilt the lower reservoir and pumped the water directly into their pipeline to Butte. It was used in Butte in this manner until 1979. After that system was discontinued, water that was not used for irrigation purposes once again was allowed to join Warm Springs Creek near the Hefner's Dam pumping station on old Cable road.

In 1992 when Deer Lodge County purchased the Anaconda Division of the Butte Water Company, the acquisition included the water rights to the Hearst Lake and Fifer Gulch drainages. At that time the Anaconda Division undertook a complete revamping of the city water supply. Several additional wells were dug in the west valley, and a huge new 3 1/2 million gallon water storage tank was built on the foothills overlooking the mouth of the former reservoir gulch. New water mains were installed throughout the city itself and the whole system was completely modernized.

After the completion of the new system, Hearst Lake once again came into the community's consciousness when the county requested the State Board of Health to change the water use classification of Hearst Lake and Fifer Gulch drainages to protect the quality of the water, in case it would once again be needed to supply the city water system. Recent trends indicating increasing population concerned county officials about future water needs, prompting the request for the change.

Since the reclassification to the A-Closed designation, hikers and motorbikers will no longer be using the 'fine wagon road' which provided a challenging day's walk for the hardy for so many years. At the lake, the masonry and stone dams constructed to raise the level of the water still stand in tribute to the talent and skill of the builders. The ruins of the brick battery house below the lower lake bear mute testimony to the artistry of those forgotten bricklayers who labored over a century ago for $2.50 per day in the mountains near Anaconda, soon to be famous as the home of the largest copper smelter in the world.

3 Phoebe

Phoebe Apperson was about seven years old when George Hearst left Missouri to go seek his fortune in the gold fields of California. The Appersons were pioneer frontier stock in Franklin county, Missouri, farming and running a general store. They were not affluent by any means, but lived comfortably enough off the land. It was Phoebe's mother's family for whom the first community in Franklin County was named, Whitmire Settlement. The Whitmires had emigrated from South Carolina to Missouri under the guidance of Daniel Boone in 1818.

Phoebe's father Randolph Walker Apperson, was from Virginia, where the family name, (sometimes spelled with an 'E',) had a long history. Phoebe was born at the farm home of her maternal grandparents on December 3, 1842. From her father, Phoebe received lessons in accounting and sums, and as a little girl she hauled buttermilk in a wagon to sell for five cents a glass to the railroad workers building the Southwestern Branch line through the area. Her father treated her like a son, and they spent much time together; she was an excellent rider and could handle a team with great competence, despite her diminutive size. A brother Elbert arrived when Phoebe was eight years old.

As a farm girl, Phoebe was taught to be self-sufficient. She could sew her own clothes, card her own wool, plant and hoe the garden, and milk the cows. She loved to read, and read every book she could lay her hands on, even those in French. Her kind heart and cheerful nature made her a great favorite with her neighbors. She attended a one-room school, to which she eventually returned as a teacher, and also attended a seminary in the adjoining county, called Steelville Academy, which was run by the Cumberland Presbyterian church. In 1859 she

Phoebe Apperson Hearst. Portrait from the Hearst Free Library Collection.

went on to teach at the Meramec Iron Works, about 30 miles from her home. The school was for children of the iron workers, and Phoebe became one of the most popular teachers. She also tutored the children of a rich mining family, where she in turn was tutored in French. She was very intelligent, and was eager to improve herself. She had many suitors, but was not seriously interested in any of the young men in her life until George Hearst came home from California, after an absence of

One room school which Phoebe attended and at which she was later a teacher.

ten years.

George began to call on Phoebe while she was teaching at the Iron Works. As previously mentioned, the Appersons were quite upset by their only daughter's interest in a man 22 years her senior, but George was persistent, and Phoebe was willing, and on June 15, 1862 the two were wed at the home of a friend in Steelville. It took several months for George to conclude his business affairs. By the time they were ready to leave, the civil war had reached Missouri, and George needed a passport to get through Union Army lines. He finally accomplished this and in late September they were able to travel by buggy to St. Louis, then by train to New York, where they boarded a steamship bound for Panama. They crossed the isthmus on a newly completed railroad, boarded the steamship *Sonora* and arrived in San Francisco on the 6th of November, 1862.

During the trip, Phoebe became friends with Mr. and Mrs. James Peck and their four children, including Janet and Orrin. Mrs. Peck took kindly interest in the young bride, and their friendship lasted a lifetime. Orrin became a familiar fixture in the Hearst household as Phoebe became his benefactress, sending him to school to study art, and Janet to study music. Orrin eventually painted a fine portrait of Phoebe which hangs in Hearst Hall at the National Cathedral School in Washington, D.C.

It wasn't until after they finally reached San Francisco that Phoebe found out she was not going to live in the mining camps and be a miner's wife. They moved into the grandest hotel in town, the newly completed Lick House. Greeted one morning soon after, with seven made-to-order silk dresses which George had ordered for his bride from Davidson's Department Store, Phoebe soon developed a taste for expensive fashions, which George happily provided.

In a short time they moved into the Stevenson House, an apartment-hotel, where on April 29, 1863, Phoebe gave birth to their only son, William Randolph. Soon after Will's birth, George bought a simple brick house on Rincon Hill, the most fashionable part of San Francisco, and settled his wife and son there. With them comfortably taken care of, George went back to the mountains in search of gold, and Phoebe devoted herself to raising her boy and taking advantage of the cultural and educational opportunities offered by the growing city.

Phoebe soon had her parents for company. George provided a nice ranch for them and her brother Elbert, and they lived very comfortably there for the rest of their lives. George was able to indulge his passion for race horses with this ranch, and in 1864 opened Bayview Racetrack at Hunter's Point, a few miles south of the heart of San Francisco.

For the ensuing years there were good times and bad times for George's mining ventures, but through them all Phoebe widened her circle of friends, broadened her knowledge of all things cultural and indulged her son William. George survived some disastrous speculations; they even had to give up the Rincon Hill House in 1874 or 1875, but after he became allied with J. B. Haggin and Lloyd Tevis, his fortunes stabilized. Phoebe was able to continue to satisfy her insatiable curiosity and she and Will proceeded to travel about and see the world.

Phoebe was disappointed at never having a little sister for

Will, and through the years she took in many young women to educate, guide and launch into society.

Will entered public school, which didn't last long, then had a private tutor who accompanied them to Europe. From his childhood, however, Phoebe wanted him to attend Harvard, the finest university in the country; and to prepare him for this at age 16 he was sent to St. Paul's School near Concord, New Hampshire. Although he roomed with Will Tevis, son of his father's business partner, he was very homesick, and it was apparent that formal methods of education were not to his liking.

During the years he was away at school, Phoebe began to devote much time and energy to charitable activities. During her many parties and entertainments, as she became acquainted with young men and women who did not have the money to advance their talents, she quietly, usually anonymously, began to make the necessary funds available to advance their education. It started modestly, but developed into a definite plan—to support the education which enabled people to help themselves.

Will's disregard for higher education eventually ended in his being sent home in disgrace from Harvard, but Phoebe's quiet interest in the education of talented young people bore much fruit through the years, and the success of hundreds of deserving people bears testimony to her generosity.

George's appointment to the U.S. Senate in 1886 moved the family to Washington, D.C. while Will was still at Harvard. Phoebe's philanthropic activities went with her. She established free kindergartens for the poor children of Washington and established the National Cathedral School for Girls.

George's health deteriorated while in Washington, where he served quietly and effectively as a representative of the state of California. His death due to cancer in his prime at age 71 was a devastating blow to Phoebe, to whom he left his entire estate. Upon her diminutive shoulders fell the burden of administering George's vast business interests, with an estate estimated at 20 million dollars. They had discussed Will's inability to manage money wisely, so by leaving everything to his wife, George knew that Phoebe would have some control over Will's spending.

Phoebe's philanthropies became more numerous and grander in scale, including an architectural plan for the building of the University of California, and many key buildings for that campus, where she was named the first woman regent.

Included in the estate, of course, were the interests in the Homestake properties in South Dakota, and the Anaconda copper mine and smelter in Montana. Phoebe had always felt great concern for the working people and their families in the towns that existed around the mines that had made the Hearsts rich. Among her plans for giving something back to these people, were public libraries for the communities of Lead, South Dakota, and Anaconda, Montana. What better way to show her affection and gratitude to these communities than by providing institutions of learning for the benefit of all, for generations yet to come? To assist in these endeavors, she needed someone she could trust to carry out her wishes. She called upon two second cousins of George's for whom she had high regard; Edward and Fred Clark, who were running a store in Fresno which had been started by their father, Austin. Austin's brothers were the cousins who had accompanied George to California in 1850.

Main sources for this chapter were:
Bonfils, Winifred Black; *The Life and Personality of Phoebe Apperson Hearst.* Friends of Hearst Castle, San Simeon; 1991.
Robinson, Judith; *The Hearsts; An American Dynasty.* U of Delaware Press, 1991.

4 Phoebe Apperson Hearst Library in Lead, South Dakota

ccording to both Mildred Fielder in 'Homestake Gold,' and Lois Miller in an article called 'Library at Lead is Monument to Philanthropist,' in the Rapid City Daily Journal, the free public library in Lead was established in 1894 in the Miners Union Opera House. Fielder says Miss Mary Jane Palethorpe was first librarian; Miller gives the honor to Mrs. Ferris. Phoebe Hearst gave the library to the city in 1894 as a Christmas present.

Two years later it moved to a room over the Hearst Mercantile on North Mill street where it stayed until it was moved into the Homestake Recreation Building when it was built in 1914. The original Hearst Mercantile, which was built in 1877, was one of the buildings condemned in 1921 when much of the business district of Lead was caving in because of inadequately supported stopes beneath the city. The business was rebuilt in 1922 farther up the street. Then on August 31, 1942, the Mercantile building burned to the ground, taking with it the main offices of the Homestake Mining Company and law offices in the west corner. Homestake had no ownership in the store since Phoebe had sold her interest in it, and many of the company records were removed before the flames completely consumed the building.

The Homestake Recreation Building was a handsome structure, with not only a permanent home for the Hearst Library, but also a lounge, club rooms, a billiard room, a swimming pool, a bowling alley and a theater. The guiding hand behind its construction was T.J.Grier, who reorganized the Homestake Company with the humanitarian beliefs of Phoebe Hearst, her agent Edward H. Clark, and with the approval of the Haggin and Tevis families. Built primarily for the use of Homestake employees, it was used and much appreciated by the whole community. Vaudeville was in vogue at the time it was built,

Martha Livingstone: Assistant in Anaconda, went on to be head librarian at Lead in 1917

and the Opera House was very popular.

The Hearst estate maintained the library after Phoebe's death in 1919, until 1925, at which time the books, art objects and equipment were all turned over to the Homestake Company. Edward Clark was president of the company and also manager of the Hearst estate, so all that was really necessary was preparing the legal papers. There was no need to move anything. For a time it was referred to as the Homestake Library.

Financial difficulties and a strike against the Homestake

Library at Lead. 1896-1914

Mine caused the closure of the recreation center and the library in July of 1972, and the Homestake Company turned the building and its contents over to the City of Lead. The library was reopened in October of that year. In January 1973 the Hearst Foundation gave a grant of $7500 to the library for operating expenses. The name was changed at that time from the Homestake Library to the Phoebe Apperson Hearst Library, and funding came from Lawrence county and the City of Lead.

On April 2, 1984, a disastrous fire, which apparently started in the area of the pipe organ under the stage of the Opera House, destroyed the building, with the exception of the library and the YMCA. The fire broke through the wall of the library in one place, and considerable smoke and water damage was caused to the magazine storage room, but the book collection was pretty well intact. The Mooring Company of San Francisco was hired to dry, clean, and deodorize the contents of the library, which were then moved to the Youthland Building at 312 W. Main. It stayed there until October of 1986, when it moved into its present location at 315 W. Main.

The Phoebe Apperson Hearst Library occupies two floors, with the Adult collection and South Dakota collection being on the street level. The children's section is downstairs, as is the George Hearst Research Room and the T.J. Grier Historical Vaults. The vaults are two cement walled rooms just off the research room, which house quite a number of documents (payroll records, ledgers, etc.) from the Homestake Mining Company dating back to the late 1800's. There are also a number of bound volumes of the *Lead Daily Call* and school enrollment records and other data pertaining to the schools in Lead dating back a number of years. These documents were found in several old warehouses and other buildings owned by the Homestake Mining Company and were donated to the mining museum. A grant was obtained in 1989 for the purposed of renovating this room and the vaults. It was dedicated on October 28, 1989.

The library still maintains the foreign language books that it has had as part of their holdings for a good number of years. These books are significant to the history of Lead as many of the early day residents came from Europe and the Scandinavian countries. The books, along with some out-of-print mining journals and books have been incorporated as part of the George Hearst Research Room.

Since 1976, funding has been solely from Lawrence county, although the city provides the building. The county budgets one lump sum which is divided among four libraries in the county. They are the only county funded libraries in South Dakota. The board of trustees consists of five local citizens, and meets every other month.

5 The Temporary Library

n August 2, 1894, Mrs. Hearst paid a visit to Anaconda, and laid the groundwork for her planned beneficence to the busy little city. She arrived on the train, and went immediately to the Montana. The smelters were producing copper around the clock, and the town was beginning to take on a look of permanence, with a number of large brick business blocks, and many fine new homes.

The announcement of her desire to build a library was warmly and enthusiastically received by the city council, and she investigated several potential sites for the building. With the intention of getting an immediate start on her project, however, Mrs. Hearst secured the use of a big brick building on the corner of Third and Cherry streets which had been used by the Company as an office building, and renovation of the structure for use as a temporary library was undertaken in the fall. On November 15, 1894, several large cases of books arrived at the depot, and the townspeople waited with great anticipation for the completion of the renovations so that the books could be moved into their temporary home.

Meanwhile, Mrs. Hearst assigned the designing of her library to New York architect, Charles Schweinfurth, who began drawing plans for a handsome structure to cost in the neighborhood of $100,000, a building to be a model of modern library construction, but also a beauty in an architectural way.

The temporary library was officially opened in spring of 1895, and the townspeople enjoyed the facility in increasing numbers. The first floor of the comfortably appointed building was devoted to a reading room containing all the leading newspapers and magazines, freely accessible to all. There were trade papers, the illustrated American weeklies, and publications in English, French and German.

On the second floor was a spacious well lighted comfortably furnished room for lounging and reading, and two side rooms with tables and chairs, outfitted for cards, chess and checkers. The tables were described as being built of burnished copper covered with green cloth. Gambling was not permitted on the premises, but for a social game, the equipment was all that could be desired. There were three dozen chairs of oak and leather, and tables throughout the building were furnished with stationery and pens so that the young men of the community could avail themselves of the opportunity to write to their loved ones 'back home.' Before too long, it was discovered that the enthusiasm engendered by the card games and checkers was not compatible with the more studious and scholarly pursuits, and the games were discontinued, with the card rooms being turned over to writing and research areas.

The larger room upstairs was outfitted with encyclopedias, dictionaries, concordances, and a fine 88 volume leatherbound set of Harpers Magazine, containing articles on nearly every subject of interest and importance.

Charles H. Babbitt, a well-known newspaperman of Washington, D.C. was Mrs. Hearst's agent in procuring books and periodicals for the libraries in Anaconda and Lead, and on a visit to Anaconda in June of 1895, he assured the locals that the Hearst Library was an absolute certainty, although Mrs. Hearst had been quite ill and had gone to Europe to rest and recuperate and would not return to this country until autumn.

Meanwhile, Richard deB. Smith had been hired by Mrs. Hearst as librarian, and he and Fred Clark, Mrs. Hearst's 'Western agent' were busy cataloging the 1100 volumes already on hand, and hoped to have them ready for circulation by July 1. A neat sign reading 'Hearst Free Library' was placed over the door, and the area immediately adjacent to the building, which had been sort of a common area used by boys and youth for football and baseball and various other raucous pastimes, was apparently fenced, thereby putting a stop to the noise and rudeness which had frequently 'shocked the ladies going to and from the library.'

The *Anaconda Standard* of July 14, 1895 reported: "Librarian Davies of Butte visited the library last week and expressed him-

Temporary Library on Cherry Street. 1895-1898

self very freely commending the work of classification and cataloging, as done by Mr. Smith, and spoke in the highest terms of praise for the collection of books."

The Standard went on to say that Librarian Smith had the cards all ready to issue, and that according to his instructions, they would be issued to all comers. There would be no guarantee or money deposit asked of those who wished to make use of the library. "Mrs. Hearst has unbounded confidence in the people of this city, and believes that they will not impose upon her generosity or abuse the privileges which she so freely gives them," the newspaper stated. Books were to be returned within two weeks, or if kept longer, had to be renewed every two weeks. "The implicit trust of Mrs. Hearst is a high compliment to the citizens of Anaconda, and to violate it would be nothing short of criminal," the article concluded.

The completed temporary library was officially opened to the public for circulation of books on July 22, 1895. Publicity on the library in the *Anaconda Standard* was frequent for the next year.

By October of that first year of operation, the boys and girls of the public schools were reported as being among the most enthusiastic patrons. The lists of new books, selected by Mr. Babbitt, were eagerly snapped up by the reading public as Mr. Smith and Mr. Clark made them available. New on the shelves for children's pleasure were the Elsie books and Mildred stories for girls; Charles Carleton Coffin's stirring tales of history; Knox's description of the Boy Travelers; the Ragged Dick set by Horatio Alger Jr.; Edward Everett Hale's stories of war on sea and land; Mrs. Burnett's famous Lord Fauntleroy and others, and the 'witty and pathetic pen pictures' of Kate Douglas Wiggins.

Older readers were waiting impatiently for W. D. Howell's books, 30 volumes of Anthony Trollope, Lew Wallace's Ben Hur, Hall Caine's books, "which have made him the latest of literary lions," Conan Doyle, J.M. Barrie, Wilkie Collins, Miss Muloch, William Black, George McDonald, and others of equal standing.

On a non-book subject, the Standard mentions in November that "Jack Martin killed a beautiful white swan yesterday at Ried's pond on Lost Creek. He brought it to Anaconda and made R. deB. Smith a present of the bird. Librarian Smith will have the specimen mounted and it will be added to his collection of Montana game at the Hearst Free Library."

Statistics for the end of November of that first year of operation show a total of 1588 books on the shelves, 1404 of which were circulating. There were 1006 card holders, circulation of 2413, and 1478 visits to the reference department. There were no losses during the month, every book taken out was returned. Books were being well taken care of and returned in good condition, and only one book was missing for the entire time the library had been open. That patron had moved to Butte, and it was hoped by the reporter that "for the sake of his peaceful conscience and this city's fair fame, he has only forgotten the book and not misappropriated it."

Librarian Richard deB. Smith resigned his position early in 1896, having carefully carried out the task which fell to his lot about one year previously. He had established the library upon a basis that was creditable to him, and elicited from Mrs. Hearst a letter of highest praise and commendation for his work, expressing also her regret for his departure and wishing him success in his new venture, whatever it might be. Smith went to the East the following week, and upon his return to Anaconda, engaged in the insurance business with Thomas F. Mahoney at 209 Main. He lived at the Montana. He was succeeded as head librarian by Fred Clark, who had moved his family to 602 Locust street. Miss Isabel Tracy was hired to assist at the library.

Patrons became very indignant when someone would fail to return a book. Darwin's 'Descent of Man' was taken by one 'Professor' T.J.Dempsey, who figured for a time as an instructor in the manly art at the Athletic Club gymnasium. Local wags felt the stolen book had a timely title as Dempsey left town rather suddenly, with some portable property from the athletic club, and owing several creditors.

The *Anaconda Standard* of March 25, 1896, provides a colorful yarn from the library, repeated here as it appeared:

'A maid of uncertain years happened into the library one day not long ago and after looking all about upstairs and down finally approached the wicket window. She was not bashful, and her figure was almost rotund.

"I was just a-thinking," said she, "that I'd like to get something to read."

"Have you got a card?" politely asked the librarian.

"No, but I thought I'd call and look over what you had."

"We have all kinds of books—fiction, history or biography, what would you like?"

"Have you any of Laura Jean Libbey's novels?"

"No m'am; but we have George Eliot's works complete. Would not one of those be better?"

"I don't like that man's style; he is too much agin the men," said she. "You might give me one of Bertha Clay's."

"Sorry m'am, but we have no books by that author."

"Well, I don't b'lieve you've got anything in here worth reading. Have you got any novels by the Duchess?"

"No m'am."

"Have you got "Fat, Fair and Forty?"

This was too much for the equanimity of the accommodating bookman, the title was so much like his client, that he burst out laughing; as he shook his head, the madam, with her nose in the air at an angle of 45 degrees, slammed the door behind her, and vowed she would never come back to this place again. "You ain't got nothin' fit to read on the shelfs." she screamed defiantly as a parting shot from the storm entry.'

Each succeeding week, patron use of the library increased, and was duly reported in the paper. At the request of lady patrons, a reading and writing room for their exclusive use was set up, giving them retirement from the throng in the general reading room.

On June 24, 1896, Mrs. Hearst visited the temporary library, and expressed herself as much gratified with what she found there. Accompanying her on this trip were Mrs. Anthony and Miss Anthony, Mrs. Robinson and son of Washington, Miss Agnes Lane of Washington, and Miss Annie Apperson of San Francisco. (Elbert's daughter.) They were enroute to California to spend the summer months.

Mrs. Hearst stated that plans for the Hearst Library building were progressing favorably, that it would be handsome and commodious; its details were engaging her personal attention and the architect who had the preparation of the plans would reach Anaconda in a few days for the purpose of examining the site and the surroundings.

An editorial in the same issue reiterated the tone of all the previous articles, pointing out that there were few reading rooms in the country where the number of visitors, in proportion to population, was as large as at the Hearst Free Library. "The Hearst Free Library will be an enduring blessing and a noble monument to the generosity of its donor; it will be one among the many splendid evidences of Mrs. Hearst's well-directed benevolence," it concluded.

Architect A. C. Schweinfurth arrived in the city in July to look over available material for the structure, and study the possibilities of the site with reference to its artistic advantages. The location on Main street had been secured in 1895, and although Mr. Schweinfurth could not give any details of the building, he was well pleased with the location, and with the local granite and foundation stone. He was also impressed with the quality of local brick. It was believed that Mrs. Hearst, after a conference in San Francisco with Mr. Schweinfurth, would have the foundation laid in the fall, and building should commence in early spring.

Coverage in the newspaper of activities at the temporary library continued, with lists of books received, and expression of gratitude to the generosity of the donor. Miss Tracy assumed the responsibilities of the head librarian, assisted by Ann Douglas, and Fred Clark and his family returned to San Francisco, where Fred continued his duties as 'Western agent.' In spring of 1897 he was back in Anaconda, ready to push the work on the new building along immediately.

There had been a vast change in plans, although the newspaper reported merely that changes in the original plans had necessitated a little delay. The fact of the matter was that after selling her shares of Anaconda stock, which meant a quarter of a million dollars less income to her per year, Phoebe decided to build a much smaller, less ostentatious institution than she had originally planned for Anaconda.

The plans of Charles Schweinfurth had been scrapped, and Phoebe turned to a young San Francisco architect, Frank S. Van Trees, for a design. Van Trees was regarded very highly in San Francisco at the time. He and Schweinfurth, who had moved West from New York City, were both affiliated with a very prestigious architectural firm in San Francisco, that of A. Page Brown, whose designs were having much impact on the city by the sea. At the time of Brown's untimely death in an accident in 1896, Van Trees seems to have taken over a number of Brown's important accounts. Perhaps Phoebe Hearst was one of them. At any rate, Van Trees did the plan for the Anaconda library, and Schweinfurth also did others for the Hearsts, including Will's Rancho del Pozo de Varona in Alameda county. Several Frank Van Trees buildings are still to be seen in San Francisco, but the Hearst Free Library in Anaconda is the only known Van Trees building in the state of Montana.

Ground was broken for the new building on June 14, 1897, and there is not another word in the *Anaconda Standard* about the work until it was completed in June of 1898.

James C. Twohy had complete superintendency of the work. Twohy was a member of the firm of Twohy Brothers, one of the prominent railroad contracting firms of the Northwest. The firm completed some of the largest railroad construction in the West, and in 1892, associated with John R. Toole, built the Butte, Anaconda and Pacific Railroad. Mr. Twohy made Anaconda his home for several years, living at 518 Locust, and eventually moved to Spokane. He must have been an efficient superintendent, as the building was completed, dedicated and open for business in one year's time.

The temporary library at Third and Cherry was closed on May 23, 1898, and books, furnishings and fixtures were moved into the new building. Fred Clark was on hand once again to supervise the move, and by June 1, books were available informally for circulation from the new library.

The old building was used by the Twentieth Century Athletic club as a clubhouse and gymnasium for several years, until purchased and refitted by the Knights of Columbus who used it for their lodge until 1950; when it was torn down to make room for the new Anaconda Central High School.

6 Building and Dedication of The New Library

The description of the official opening and dedication of the new building covered the entire first page of the feature section of the *Anaconda Standard*, which at that time was one of the leading newspapers in the West. Arrangements for the reception for Mrs. Hearst were in the hands of a committee presided over by Judge Theodore Brantly.

The formal ceremony was at the Margaret Theater at 8:30 on Saturday, June 11, l898. The theater was filled to capacity for the event, upstairs and down, with quite a few standing. There were 30 persons on the stage, including city officials, the ladies of the reception committee, the local clergy, and the speakers for the evening, who had been strictly limited to 7 minutes apiece. The program opened with the orchestra playing "Stars and Stripes." J.H. Durston acted as Master of Ceremonies, and in the words of the Anaconda Recorder, Anaconda's weekly newspaper, 'performed his duties in the happy manner which always mark his appearances in public.'

The first speaker on the program was the honorable Robert B. Smith, Governor of Montana, who expressed the congratulations of all the citizens of Montana to Anaconda, for securing such a handsome library. "Some of the grandest cities in ancient times are remembered particularly on account of the libraries they possessed," the governor stated. Of Anaconda's library, he said, "I had the pleasure this evening of observing the building. It is a magnificent structure, a perfect work of art; so perfect, indeed, that if it were smaller, it might be worn appropriately on your shirt bosom—it is a gem."

At the conclusion of the governor's comments, the audience joined in singing "America." Judge Brantly then made a scholarly address, representing the county of Deer Lodge, in which he suggested the people of Anaconda could best show their appreciation of this beautiful gift by using it.

Colonel Timothy O'Leary, on behalf of the city council, read the resolution passed by that body, and added appreciative remarks on the large generosity of the gift. To Mrs. Hearst he directed a flowery description of Lake Hearst as " a reservoir that gives growth and beauty to our trees and lawns, and health, vigor and vitality to our people," and compared it with the library as " a reservoir whence will flow out streams of pure, healthful literature to fructify and strengthen the intellectual life of our people."

After another musical presentation by the orchestra, the honorable Elmer D. Matts, a lawyer with offices in the bank building, was called upon to speak on behalf of the people-at-large of the city. He paid brief but honest tribute to Senator Hearst and his life's work in the great West, and expressed the gratitude of the people of Anaconda to Mrs. Hearst. "If there was one thing the city of Anaconda needed, it was a free public library," Mr. Matts said. "A few years ago the nucleus of the present library was started in the old building, and today it finds its home in the most magnificent building in the state of Montana."

Interrupted several times by applause, Mr. Matts upheld his reputation as an orator. He continued: "...This library is not alone patronized by the children who go to our schools, and that is its best feature, but it is patronized by the men who toil at the foundry, in the smelter, upon the railroad, or in the stores and offices of this city." He concluded his remarks by saying "We are not unmindful that it is in memory of a man whose public services are a part of the history of our country, whose private work is known wherever the miner's pick has sounded. We are not forgetful either that it was largely through his instrumentality that the foundations were laid for the present prosperity of the city of Anaconda. We shall always remember the name of Senator Hearst whenever we look at this library, which perpetuates his memory."

The chairman read congratulatory telegrams from Governor Budd of California, the faculties of Montana University at Missoula and the Agricultural College at Bozeman, the

Architect's sketch from Anaconda Standard, *December 19, 1897*

Montana Supreme Court, and the trustees of the Butte Free Library. After another musical rendition, Mrs. Hearst was introduced, to a thunderous ovation, and her brief address, as reported in the Standard, follows:

"As the absorbing interest of my husband's life was mining, with its collateral industries, and his love of the great West and all the personal friendships in it a joy until his last day, my son and myself sought some way of adding to the pleasure of the people who are spending their lives in the development of the material and other interests of this mining region. We could think of no more lasting and wide spreading influence for good than a library, and we take great satisfaction in giving you what we hope will be a help to all as the years go on. In view of the great advance in the arts, with the constantly changing economic conditions, and in the vast discoveries in science, it becomes a necessity of individual and civic advancement to keep abreast of modern thought and investigation, and the library is the common ground for this preparation.

"Then for the solace and intellectual pleasure of those out of the wearing strife of the day's affairs, the library will be a blessing, while for the young who get their stimulus and lifelines

Main reading room.
Photo courtesy of the Montana Historical Society

through the unconscious tuition of their environment, it will be a potent factor."

At the conclusion of Mrs. Hearst's remarks, the audience joined in a rousing rendition of "The Red, White and Blue," and the formal services closed.

Upon leaving the theater, the people proceeded up Main street to the new library building. The interior had been beautifully decorated with flowers for the occasion. Directly under the portrait of Mrs. Hearst stood a vase of carnations. Beneath the portrait of Senator Hearst was a stand upon which was a profusion of flowers. At this stand Mrs. Hearst took her station upon her arrival. She greeted the townspeople with a shake of the hand, a smile, and a few kind words, and they passed out of the side door. The reception lasted nearly an hour. Mrs. Hearst was assisted by the ladies of the reception committee.

As the description of the library in the pages of the *Anaconda Standard* is particularly fine, it is included here in its entirety.

BOOKS IN THEIR NEW HOME

In a commanding position on Main street, with lines of impressive, classical beauty stands the Hearst free public library, a gift to the people of Anaconda from Mrs. Phoebe Hearst. The first impression one receives is of massive substantiality, an effect which is heightened by the striking Grecian purity of outline and the almost severe use of ornamentation which by itself would give an impression of stiffness were it not for the graceful strength imparted to the design by the great spreading arches of the windows. The building is the best type of library structure, and has not its equal in Montana and will compare favorably with any public building in the West.

The building is erected on one of the choicest sites in the city, a lot 150 by 140 at the corner of Main and Fourth streets. The building itself is 72 by 75, facing on Fourth and situated in the middle of the lot, giving room for a fine lawn. The building is a two-story structure with a basement and a trussed roof and the material of which it is composed is selected pressed brick, the foundations and trimmings being of gray Gregson granite.

The facade is exceptionally pure in design and impressive in appearance. Eight granite steps, 38 feet long, lead up to a deep portico, the entablature resting on two massive granite columns carrying Corinthian capitals, the effect of which is harmoniously followed out throughout the rest of the facade and the other sides of the building by pilasters. Between the pilasters, which rest on the basement walls of dressed Gregson granite, are the spreading arches of the large plate glass windows of the first floor, while the square windows of the second story give an impression of massive substantiality which is contrasted and relieved by the graceful lines of the Corinthian caps of the pilasters supporting a heavy architrave of copper. Upon the frieze, which is left severely plain, rests the heavy copper cornice in the usual conventional lines.

The portico with its columns 27 feet high, takes up half of the facade and presents a rich appearance with its heavy copper trimmings. The entrance to the library is through large double oak doors above which is an arched marble tablet bearing the inscription "Hearst Free Library."

The doors open into a vestibule, richly yet simply finished in quartered oak and then through two large swinging doors the library proper is reached, which occupies the whole of the first floor with the exception of a private office for the librarian. As on the outside so in the inside, there cannot be perceived a single discordant line or an inharmonious feature or detail of design. Floods of light pour in from the great arched windows and it is caught up and subdued by the neutral tinting of the walls and ceiling, a provision which is appreciated by readers. The east side of the main floor is partitioned off by a bronze railing beyond which are the book shelves of japanned steel conveniently situated with relation to the librarian's delivery desk. The rest of the floor space is given up to newspaper and magazine racks and reading tables.

Beauty and utility are gracefully blended in the design of this part of the building. The effect of simple lines, of rich yet plain finishings, the entire absence of meaningless ornamentation, the rigid observance of the canons of good architectural taste in the smallest details, produce an impression that is not soon forgotten and reflects the greatest credit on the architect and those who so skillfully gave form and substance to his ideas.

The main floor is lighted by ten large glass windows 7 1/2 by 10 feet and seven smaller ones, and in the evening 180 incandescents pendant from rich brass chandeliers throw a pleasing light through frosted globes. The floor is laid in maple finished in oil. All of the finishing is in quarter-sawed white oak, harmonizing perfectly with the neutral color of the walls. One of the most pleasing features of the first floor design is the great fireplace on the south side with its massive oak mantel reaching two-thirds of the way to the ceiling.

The blankness of the wall spaces is pleasantly broken by pictures of more than ordinary interest and art value. There are portraits of the late Senator Hearst and Mrs. Hearst and a number of oils, engravings and photogravures. In one corner is a well executed bust of Senator Hearst in marble. A burntwood portrait of Agassiz is worthy of particular notice.

The second floor of the building is carried on steel I beams, supported by three columns, and is reached by a stairway at the northwest corner of the building. Stairs lead to a large hall from which open the different rooms of the second floor. A rich heavy baluster marks the stairway landing. From the hall one looks out through large square windows on the portico and the walls are hung with several engravings and oils. Wide double doors open from the hall into the two large reference rooms which, with two writing rooms, make up the divisions of the second floor. The women's writing room occupies the northwest corner and is cozily fitted up with writing tables, easy lounging chairs and couches, while water colors and engravings give the room an added attractiveness and three large square windows furnish plenty of light. From these windows a view of unexcelled beauty of the surrounding snow-capped mountains is obtained.

The reference library and women's reading room is reached by a door from the writing room in addition to the large double doors from the hall. It is a large, well lighted room occupying in space about two-thirds of the west side of the second floor, and is finished and fitted up in a style similar to that prevailing throughout the building. A large reference library is found on the shelves along the partition of white oak, and magazine racks are scattered here and there near the reading tables, while large easy chairs show that comfort as well as utility has been consulted in fitting up the room.

On the east side of the second floor are the men's writing room and the reading room, with a large reference library. The reading room is larger than the one on the other side, but the same general plan of furnishing is observed. The partition between the two reading rooms is movable, so that if the necessity should arise the two rooms could be thrown into one large lecture room. As on the first floor, every available wall space has its engraving, pastel, photogravure or oil, forming a well selected nucleus for an art gallery. Upon both floors such conveniences as cloak rooms and closets have not been overlooked.

The heating, lighting and ventilating plants are complete in every respect. There are 320 incandescent lights scattered throughout the building, the light softened for the eyes by frosted globes. The ventilation of the building is as near perfect as modern mechanism can make it, the air being changed automatically every 20 minutes.

Taken in its ensemble the Hearst Free Public Library building is as perfect as can be found anywhere. The ground was broken for the construction of the library July 28, 1897, and the library was thrown open to the public June 1, 1898. There was no contract work at all in connection with the construction of the building and only the best material was used in the work. The architect was Frank S. Van Trees of San Francisco, and J. C. Twohy of this city had entire superintendency of the work of erecting the building.

By the end of November, there were 4,094 cardholders at the library, and librarian Miss Isabel Tracy reported a brisk business.

Just before Christmas, there was a display of great interest in the window of the Copper City Commercial Company, consisting of a memorial shield which had been designed for the people of Anaconda to give to Mrs. Hearst as a token of their appreciation. The shield was made of copper, silver and gold from the Anaconda mine in Butte, reduced at the Anaconda smelter. The designs on the frame were the Montana state flower, the bitterroot, and the mountain pine. The 18 x 12 silver plate occupying the center of the shield showed the library building with Literature holding up the Lamp of Knowledge, and below as a foundation, the insignia of the various departments. The frame was of bronze and overall size was 48 x 30 inches. In the illumination of the initial letters in the headline and text, the California poppy was used. Engraved upon the plate were the resolutions passed by the city council and presented to Mrs. Hearst at the Dedication. The engraving was from the original design drawn by Charles T. Malcomson (an electrician living at 123 E. Park.) The work was executed by the Gorham Manufacturing company, for the C.D. Peacock company. The shield was produced to express to Mrs. Hearst the love and gratitude which "is graven upon the hearts of Anaconda's people and will live forever in the hearts of their children, and their children's children."

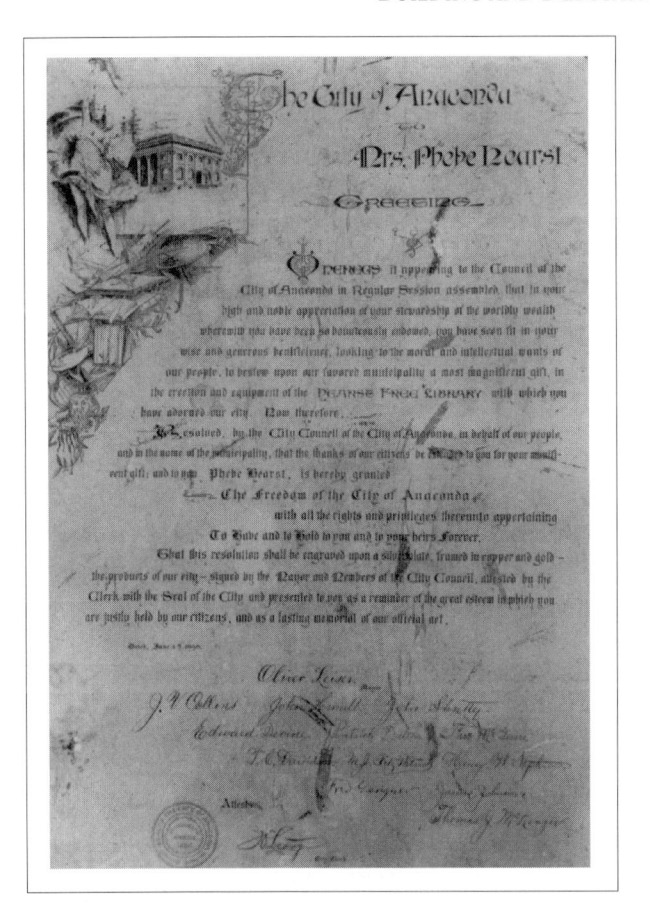

From a photograph of the Memorial Shield, presented to Mrs. Hearst as a token of appreciation.

It was viewed in the store window by hundreds of Anacondans, but it was 10 months later that city clerk Joe Peters received word from Fred Clark that Mrs. Hearst was again home in San Francisco and ready to receive the testimonial gift.

In January, 1900, the *Anaconda Standard* observed that Anacondans were fictionalists because "last year they read 28,778 stories, some of which had morals tied to their tales and some of which had not. They are geographers and historians, because they perused 2,947 volumes of geography and history. They are devotees of literary miscellany, because they consumed 803 books of that stuff. They have a care for the useful arts because they investigated 568 works on that subject. They have a high appreciation of the poetical license...because 550 tomes of rhyme, good, bad and indifferent were sought out by them and criticized: They cannot be ignorant of the beauties of natural science, because they took liberties with the mysteries entertained in no less than 516 works on that deeply absorbing affair. They must hold some cards in spades at the twin game of social science and philosophy because they made a record of 304 separate and distinct dissertations thereupon. They may lay just claim to having dabbled in the fine arts because a people cannot toy with 170 authorities on that subject and remain ignorant. They have at least a smattering of theology because it is not possible to digest 142 expositions of the unknowable without finding out something about it. They have felt the stimulating influence of Epictetus, because on philosophy they have considered 140 counsels. And lastly, they are not lop-sided specialists, hobbyists or single-subject cranks, because they have taken heed unto the seepings of diversity from the footprints of 109 steps in the great bog of general literature."

Miss Anne Whitley had succeeded Miss Tracy as librarian by this time, assisted by Miss Latham, and the library was open each day of the week from 10 o'clock in the morning until 10 o'clock at night.

Miss Latham in turn succeeded Miss Whitley, who returned to California, and after a brief stay in the position, resigned it when she married in the spring of 1901. Miss Elizabeth Thomson, one of the teachers in the high school, who had been connected with the Anaconda schools for several years, was appointed to fill the position by Fred Clark, who came to town to make the appointment. Fred was on his way to Deadwood and Lead, South Dakota, where he was to meet Mrs. Hearst on her way from the East, to look after her interests in the Black Hills. Bob Emmons had been acting assistant, and was appointed to continue in that position. "You'd better let me appoint a man," said Fred to Mrs. Hearst. "The girls seem to treat it as a marriage bureau."

7 Library Turned Over to City, 1903

Urban legend has it that Mrs. Hearst turned the library over to the city in 1903 because the socialist city council sent her a bill for taxes, supposedly figuring that since she was paying the salaries and buying the books for a building she had built, she might as well pay taxes too. The lots were indeed assessed to Mrs. Hearst, but upon complaint of her attorney, J. R. Boardman, the board decided the lots should not be assessed at all, being exempt as public property under state law.

There had been talk as early as 1901 that the building would be turned over to the city, so the tax bill may or may not have been a factor in her decision to give the library to the people of Anaconda at this particular time. It is a fact that the pressures of her benefactions were beginning to weigh heavily upon her by 1903, and by May of 1904, she had withdrawn from all her philanthropic activities, causing great consternation to all, including the University of California.

There had been financial reverses that played a part in her decision, including the drain of large amounts into Will's campaign when he was elected to congress, and his ill-fated bid for the presidential nomination from the democratic convention scheduled in the spring of 1904. But the main factor in her decision was that she felt it was time for many of her charities to become self sufficient or seek other donors, and in her desire not to show favoritism, she cut everything.

It was a tough decision she made, but basically, she was a one-woman foundation. She had no one to advise her on her philanthropic ventures. She understood the needs of all the beneficiaries of her philanthropy, and believed it was time for them to start relying on their own initiative to keep going. This was not the end of her charity, but once having made her point, she stuck to it, and went off to Europe for some rest.

By 1901 the eight hour day at the smelting works had had an impact on library use. Library officials reported that many young men were regular visitors, spending their spare hours in the library reading up on technical subjects, as well as an occasional dip into the field of romance. Although not particularly fashionable, the people who visited the Anaconda library were not idle men seeking a place of shelter and warmth, as was common even then in the libraries of larger cities, but rather were men, women and children who came to read intelligently, for both amusement and instruction.

It was estimated that rarely less than 200 people per day took advantage of the reading room on the main floor, while about 100 per day were counted upstairs in the reference department. By December of 1901, 7,580 cards had been issued to residents enabling them to borrow books from the circulating collection. This collection was enlarged twice a year, when several hundred volumes would be received.

One of the most interesting occurences in the history of Anaconda politics came with the election, in April 1903, of the entire slate of socialist candidates for city offices. The mayor, treasurer, and police magistrate were all socialists, as well as the aldermen in the fourth, fifth and sixth wards. The new council, besides the three socialist aldermen, included 3 republicans and 6 democrats. In retrospect, the 3 republicans were probably even more amazing than the three socialists.

The newly elected mayor, John W. Frinke, was a cigar maker by trade, being associated with Richard B. Peckham in that business. A resident of Anaconda since 1894, he was a handsome, athletic man who played baseball on local teams, was a fan of all outdoor sports, and was a leader in the movement to get the city common for a public playground. He always took a great interest in its development as a center for children's activities. He was well thought of by his fellow Anacondans, and seems to have been held by them in high esteem.

To this group of city officials, then, did Mrs. Hearst turn over the facilities of the Hearst Free Library in 1903. Referred to by the *Anaconda Standard* as the most useful and expensive gift presented to any municipality in the West during the year, the offer was made by Mrs. Hearst through Mr. James C. Hooe of Washington, D.C. The letter, addressed to the mayor and city council read:

Anaconda, Montana
December 1, 1903

To the Honorable Mayor and Councilmen of the
City of Anaconda, Montana

Dear Sirs:

I am directed by Mrs. Phebe [sic] A. Hearst to present to the city of Anaconda, the land and building known as the Hearst free library, together with all books and equipment, the terms of your city's acceptance to be that it shall maintain the same as a free public library for the use of the citizens of Anaconda.

This library building was erected by Mrs. Hearst in memory of her husband George Hearst, a United States senator from the state of California, and who for many years had large interests in your community, and she maintained the same at her own expense since and before the completion of this building.

Mrs. Hearst feels that the time has come for this library to become the property of the city of Anaconda and be cared for and controlled by its citizens, and in presenting the same with her well-known expressions of good will to the people of your city, I am authorized to say there will be no abatement of her interest in the library work, and she asks that the city kindly grant her permission to send to the library books of the value of $1000 annually for a period of 3 years.

With assurances of Mrs. Hearst's continued interest in this work, and acknowledging her appreciation of the manner in which this library has been patronized by the city, I am, very respectfully yours,

James C. Hooe For Mrs. Phebe A. Hearst

Library about 1913. Balustrade removed from roof in 1947.

Mr. Hooe met with the mayor and several of the prominent citizens of the community while here, and all expressed appreciation of the splendid gift, immediately indicating for the most part that the gift would be accepted in the spirit in which it was given.

Mayor Frinke did not hesitate to say that he was in favor of taking the library on the terms offered by Mrs. Hearst, and though he admitted to have not given it a lot of thought at the moment, he was of the opinion it should be turned over to a non-partisan board of trustees, who should have full control, and it should be kept out of politics.

The first meeting of the council to draw up an ordinance outlining the acceptance and governance of the library came across like a three ring circus in the Standard. The proposed ordinance, of which several different versions were hashed over and discussed at great length, were reported in detail, and were obviously very amusing to the reporter; to the extent that a week later, an editorial appeared, stating that the ordinance which had finally been proposed involving city ownership of the Hearst Free library had been carefully and intelligently discussed and that this splendid gift, if it were to come at all, would come in such a manner as to make its management and use of the utmost service to all citizens.

It provided for the levy and collection of a 1 mill tax, the proceeds of which would constitute a library fund. The general tax of one mill was the limit allowed by state law through a general levy. The editor concluded his piece by saying Mayor Frinke took up the matter in a commendable way and that he and his associates in the council had sought to act with spirited prudence in the preparation of the ordinance now to be presented to their townsmen.

In April 1904 the voters of Anaconda accepted the library ordinance by about ten to one.

During the early discussions on the proposed ordinance, Mayor Frinke made some astute observations. He suggested that from his study of libraries he had ascertained that the farther the government of the library was kept from city hall politics the better it would be for the library. He made it very clear that if he should have the appointment of trustees for the library they would be competent men, who would not be swayed by every political breeze. "I will appoint such men as this council will not turn down," said the mayor.

True to his word, Mayor Frinke came up with an outstanding group for the library's first board of trustees. The organizational meeting held on June 18, 1904 at the library, was called to order by Mayor Frinke with the purpose of effecting a permanent organization. He stated that he believed he had made no mistake in his selection of the board of trustees, and repeated his hope that it would be kept out of politics, and always be a credit to the city of Anaconda.

Elected president of the board was E. P. Mathewson. The vice president was George B. Winston; secretary, H. A. Denny. Other trustees were M. B. Greenwood and F. V. Hurley.

The existing officials of the library were retained, those being Miss Elizabeth Thomson, librarian; Miss Martha E. Livingstone, assistant; and John Fee, janitor. Preliminary plans for the running of the library were laid out. All bills had been paid up to June 1, and Mrs. Hearst had promised to buy books for the next three years.

8 The Board of Trustees and It's Illustrious First Chairman

Chosen for their astuteness in business, their interest in the community, and their respect for the institution so recently turned over to the city of Anaconda, the first board of trustees was a prestigious group in anybody's book. Frank V. Hurley was the manager of the Copper City Commercial Company' grocery and meat department, and he served on the board until 1907.

Henry A. Denny, who was elected secretary at that first meeting, was foreman of the Job Room at the *Anaconda Standard*, and the original minutes are in his meticulous hand. Mr. Denny served until he left Anaconda in 1907.

Marcellus B. Greenwood was vice president and manager of the Daly Bank and Trust Company. Before coming to Anaconda as a member of the newly organized banking firm of Daly, Donohue and Greenwood, which firm was later succeeded by the Daly Bank & Trust Company, Mr. Greenwood served a long and honorable term at the Batavian Bank in LaCrosse, Wisconsin. During a visit to St. Paul, Minnesota in September 1905, Mr. Greenwood was stricken ill and died, much to the consternation of his friends and family in Anaconda, and his death prompted the entering of the following resolution into the minutes of the library board:

> The board of trustees of the Hearst public library, desiring to express their sorrow over the death of Marcellus B. Greenwood, who was a valued member of the board from the time of its organization, and their high esteem of his splendid traits of character, order that these resolutions be spread upon the records of the board and that a copy be sent to the bereaved family:
> Resolved: That in the death of Mr. Greenwood this

board has lost a member whose wise council was at all times helpful; whose complete sympathy with the purposes of the library rendered him at all times an earnest worker in the development of the institution; whose fine traits of character made him esteemed as an officer of the library and as a man.

Resolved: That we testify to our appreciation of his services as a member of the board of trustees and as a citizen of Anaconda who was ever ready to aid in any worthy cause for the benefit of the community, and in our high esteem of his personal worth.

Resolved: That we extend to his widow and two sons the assurance of our sympathy with them in their bereavement, in which, as his friends, we share.

Out of respect to Mr. Greenwood, the library was closed at noon on the day of the funeral, which was held in LaCrosse, and stayed closed until the next morning.

George Bickerton Winston, at the time of his appointment to the board was a lawyer, with offices at the Petritz Block. He had been admitted to the Montana bar in 1884, having come here from Missouri. He was Anaconda's first city attorney, and also the first city clerk. He also was the first assistant county attorney for old Deer Lodge county, before Powell county was taken from it and before Anaconda was made the county seat. In 1889 he was a member of the constitutional convention which assembled in Helena to draw up the constitution for the state. In 1904 he was elected to his first term as judge for the third judicial district, which included Deer Lodge, Powell, and Granite counties, so his tenure on the library board was brief, due to his other commitments, but he did have the honor of being one of the members of that first board of trustees, and it's first vice president. He was replaced by Mr. C. A. Tuttle, prominent local undertaker and county commissioner.

Elected chairman of the first board of trustees was Edward Payson Mathewson. Affectionately known to the community as 'E.P.,' he had come to Anaconda in 1902 to manage the smelter. He started his career as an assayer for the Pueblo Smelting and Refining company in Colorado, and after his arrival in Anaconda

E. P. Mathewson

he played a leading role in the development of the Anaconda Reduction Works.

During his 14 years in Anaconda he was a participant in almost every civic event that went on, being a charter member and first president of the Anaconda Rotary club, a life member of the Anaconda Gun club, and an active participant in the sport of curling. He was pictured in the 1911 *Anaconda Standard* with the other members of his 'rink' who had just won the Mathewson Cup. His team members included George Jackson, W. A. Bower, and Warren Jenny, who also served as a member of the library board from 1909 to 1916.

E.P. was instrumental in the establishment of Washoe Park and the city common, and several of the playgrounds throughout the city, funding for which he arranged by pledging the Company to match every dollar that was put up by local businessmen for the observance of Independence Day in 1907. After the celebration expenses were paid, a neat surplus remained, and this, with the company's contribution, made up the fund to be devoted to playgrounds.

He was one of the organizers of the Anaconda Club, which maintained club rooms at the Montana, and on January 3, 1905, he and Mrs. Mathewson led the grand march at the first annual ball. He was the main speaker in behalf of that organization at a farewell party for J.W. Dobbins, manager of the hotel, upon that gentleman's departure for Seattle in 1907.

An auspicious event presaging the beginning of a new age occurred on August 16, 1907, with the launching of the first power boat on Georgetown Lake, the 'Lotus;' an 18 foot steel gasoline launch built by the Michigan Steel Boat Company, powered by a Detroit engine, and skippered, of course, by 'Admiral' E.P. Mathewson. The only difficulty encountered on the voyage was precipitated when the bottle of champagne, broken on the bow for the christening of the new craft, also broke the pennant staff, so the craft officially slid into the water with the flags fluttering from the stern. The launching was immortalized by a caricature drawn by John C. Terry of the *Anaconda Standard*, which hung for many years in the club room of the Anaconda Club.

In 1911, E.P. was the main speaker at the commencement exercises for Anaconda High School at the Margaret Theater. The class was the largest in the history of the school up to that time, with 26 graduates. Of the class, 20 were girls, 6 were boys, and the valedictory address was given by Lester Dragstedt, who went on to be a world-famous surgeon and physiologist.

E.P.'s civic affairs were statewide. According to Frank Smith of Helena, he was instrumental in development of the State Fair. He was elected first president of the Montana Good Roads Congress in 1912, and the State Automobile Association, and pursued the campaign for better roads for Montana with great enthusiasm. He was also a member of the commission which chose sites for the state fish hatcheries at Anaconda and at Somers on Flathead Lake.

Great forward strides in the production of copper were made during his tenure, with the invention and implementation of the slime concentrator and a larger leaching plant increasing production by about 16%. By 1913 about 3,000 men were employed and the payroll was the greatest it had ever been in Anaconda history. Not only 'on the hill,' but also downtown, the building boom had a great impact on the local economy, with the $200,000 spent on building during the year, $147,800 was for residences. Also recorded that year was the complete victory in the U.S. Supreme Court of the Company in the 'Bliss suit,' commonly known as the 'smoke case.' Mathewson had spent many hours on the witness stand in that long drawn out litigation, in which many farmers in the valley had complained of the smoke from the smelters killing their livestock and contaminating their lands.

The planting of a herd of elk west of Anaconda was another of E.P.'s projects. In April of 1914 he reported the successful transplanting of 24 head of healthy elk near Silver lake, with a small amount of money left over to start the fund to bring in more elk the following year.

'Special privilege' caused him some embarrassment in June of that year, however. Needing to look up some information in the upstairs reference room at the library, which was closed for renovation, he obtained a key from the custodian and went upstairs to do some reading. Painters were busy in the room, so E.P. found his book, retired quietly to the corner and proceeded with his project. For an hour or so he was completely absorbed in his work. When he finally closed the book and looked up, he discovered he had been painted in. To get out, he would have to leave large number 11 tracks over the freshly finished floor. Ever resourceful, he tried the windows, found one open, and let himself down the fire escape, landing safely on the green lawn below. Needless to say, the escapade did not get reported in the minutes of the next meeting of the board of trustees. What did get reported were more routine activities like appearing before the city council in behalf of the library when it was necessary to ask for more money to operate the institution.

The regular monthly shoot of the Gun Club at Nell Park (Cedar Park Homes now occupies this site) in June 1914 drew shooters from Butte and Deer Lodge as well as Anaconda to shoot for Panama-Pacific Exposition prizes provided by E.P. Mathewson.

During his tenure in Anaconda, E.P. often received proposals for positions offering more salary than what he was making here, but life in Africa or Australia and other remote places did not interest him. Then one day in the summer of 1916, a representative of the British-American Nickel corporation of Toronto came to see him, requesting him to recommend a manager for their nickel plant in Canada. Nickel was of great interest to E.P.; he recommended several names, but the gentleman did not seem enthusiastic over any of them. "If you would make it an object to me, I might take the job myself," E.P. said, half in jest. "That's just what I came out here for," the man replied. The offer made was so good, he could not refuse.

Anaconda's farewell to E.P. Mathewson was unprecedented in the town's history and has never been equalled. The shifts at the smelter and foundry were arranged so that all the men could be present at a ceremony in front of the general office building, at which E.P. was presented with a solid gold loving cup and a painting by Montana's popular cowboy artist, Charles M. Russell. The cup was engraved:

> PRESENTED TO
> EDWARD PAYSON MATHEWSON
> BY HIS
> FRIENDS AND FELLOW-WORKERS
> ANACONDA, MONTANA
> OCT. 14, 1916

The painting was of a vast herd of buffalo fording the Missouri river with the colorful hills and buttes in the background. To Mrs. Mathewson, the men presented a magnificent diamond lavalliere and diamond cluster ring in a platinum setting.

At a special meeting at the carpenters hall, members of Local 88 presented him with a solitaire diamond stickpin and receiving tray as a special memento of the affection he had won from the carpenters. He was referred to as "the best member Local 88 ever had."

The Anaconda gun club, along with Life membership, presented the Mathewsons with a solid silver tea service in recognition of the prosperity of the club and the advancement of the sport under Mr. Mathewson's leadership and inspiration.

The Anaconda Club, in their clubrooms at the Montana, held a special smoker for the original founder of the club. He was presented with a solid silver plate engraved with the words, 'Anaconda Club, Anaconda, Montana. This certifies that Edward Payson Mathewson is hereby granted a life membership with the title of Chief Duck Hunter. Oct. 9, 1916.' E.P. had often been master of ceremonies at the Annual Duckfest, and he was urged to return to Montana always the first week of September for the opening of duck season.

At a banquet at the Montana the night before his departure, more than 250 people crowded into the room to pay tribute to his community leadership for the past 14 years. A glee club from Butte sang several original numbers including "We'll always keep a light a burning in the window of the smelter on the hill." The businessmen of the community presented the Mathewsons a silver tea service and diamond rings. W.M. Montgomery, speaking on behalf of the business people, was quoted by the Standard as saying, "By your guidance, opposing interests have been harmonized; confidence has been established among those engaged in various business and professional callings. More than this, by your wisdom and integrity of purpose, you have established a perfect confidence between the residents of this city and the great corporation whose works and operations have grown to such mammoth proportions under your skillful direction. By virtue of that confidence, inspired by your wholesome optimism, this city has grown from Anaconda the camp, the temporary stopping place, to Anaconda, the beautiful little city of homes, whose corporate limits must be extended to accommodate those who desire to dwell among us."

The Rotary Club meeting at which E.P. was presented with a watchfob and honorary life membership was the largest in the local club's history up to that time. The fob was designed by jeweler Max Hammerslough, and featured the emblematic wheel of the club, with a large diamond at the hub. The words 'Anaconda,' and 'Rotary,' and the initials 'E.P.M.' were rendered in letters of gold and it was a fine specimen of the jeweler's art.

Frederick Laist had been chosen to succeed Mr. Mathewson as head of the smelter and he paid tribute to E.P.'s ability to mix with all classes and hold their good will. "Mr. Mathewson has told me that now I will have to learn to curl and shoot ducks," he said. "Well, I will try to do both and run the smelter on the side."

The whole town turned out to see the Mathewsons off on the train, bound for Toronto. They were escorted from their home at 422 Hickory by two bands, the businessmen, and school children in a long line of march. On both sides of Main street the crowd was gathered in deep lines that followed the car to the depot where 6,000 or 7,000 people joined in the most spontaneous demonstration ever given in Anaconda.

The campaign E.P. had started to build an employees club for the workers at the smelter came to a halt with his departure, and it was 34 years before the Company realized it was a really good idea and built clubs for the employees at Anaconda and Great Falls.

In 1926 E. P. became professor of administration of mineral industries at the University of Arizona in Tucson. Dr. Mathewson's genial ways, bubbling good humor and never-ceasing kindness of heart made him immensely popular in Tucson, fairly idolized by the students on campus, who declared him 'the biggest wildcat of them all.' They presented him with a life pass to University athletic contests and gave him a stein with his name on it as a token of their appreciation of his services in connection with raising funds for a new stadium.

In June 1937 he took leave of absence from the university to become superintendent for construction of a lead smelter in Hong Kong. The war stopped the development work planned by the mining company with which he was connected and in 1938 he returned to Tucson.

Word of his death there in July 1948 brought sorrow to this community which he had served so enthusiastically and well. E. P. Mathewson received many honors during his lifetime, but probably none more heartfelt than the farewell demonstration from the people of Anaconda. No man in the history of the town, probably even including Marcus Daly, was held in higher esteem by his fellow townsmen.

9 Some Other Board Members of Note

Mr. Mathewson served on the board of trustees as its very effective chairman for 12 years.

Upon his departure, Edwin B. Catlin was elected president of the board. He had been a members since his appointment in 1908, and served for 25 years. A leader in many civic enterprises, Mr. Catlin worked enthusiastically in numerous educational, civic and social activities besides the library.

He had come to Anaconda from Syracuse along with J. H. Durston to form up the *Anaconda Standard* when Marcus Daly decided he needed a first class newspaper in his new town. Originally a printer, Catlin became manager of commercial printing and merchandising at the paper, and was a member of the Typographical Union, secretary of the Theosophical Society, and a member of the Anaconda Club and Country club. His patriotic endeavors were evidenced by his popularity as a speaker for the Liberty Loan drives during the war. He was a gifted speaker and writer; often called upon to write resolutions, and deliver eulogies at funerals.

Other trustees of special note through the years include William K. Dwyer, who was appointed to the board by Mayor McKenzie in l907. He was, at the time, the superintendent of schools, a position which he held from 1905 until 1944. Mr. Dwyer had come to Anaconda from Butte in 1904 to be principal of Anaconda High School. While in Butte, he had studied law in the office of Peter Breen, and was an instructor in Butte High School.

Professor Dwyer received his early education in Ireland, where he was born in County Cork in 1870, His father was principal of schools in Castletown-Brere, so his interest in school administration may have developed early in his life. He graduated from St. Michael College in County Kerry and St. Patrick college in Tipperary. After coming to the United States in 1891, he attended St. Mary's in Baltimore where he received a Bachelor of Arts and Master of Arts degree in 1896. Then came post-graduate work in constitutional law, history, and education at the University of Chicago. He worked for Western Electric and attended night school at Lake Forest prior to his move to Butte in 1902.

Professor Dwyer filled the position as vice-chairman of the library board for several years. He was highly regarded in the state as an educator, serving as director for Montana of the National Education Association. He was also a member of the Anaconda Club and the Knights of Columbus, among his other civic activities. He died on May 9, 1950, at the family home at 505 Hickory, after serving as a trustee for 31 years.

Those early board members took quite an interest in books being purchased for the library. In 1921 Professor Dwyer recommended that a book called *The Green Bough* should be removed from the library because of its 'insiduously immoral attack on the sacredness of the family relation.' In 1918 the trustees all read *General Smutt's Message to South Wales*, and 'heartily approving of its concise and forceful statement of the significance of the world war as being not so much a clash of arms as a conflict between righteous spiritual ideals and aims, on the one side, and brutally materialistic aims on the other side,' voted to purchase 500 copies of the address for free distribution to the public. Obviously, censorship was not the big issue in libraries that it is today! During that year, trustee Frank Kennedy was also asked to review Trotsky's *Bosheviki and the World Peace*, before it was purchased for the library.

Mr. Kennedy was a pioneer of Anaconda, having arrived in 1887 to fill a clerical position with the Anaconda Copper Mining Company. Later he went into business as the King and Kennedy Store, which handled a full line of books, stationary, cigars and tobacco. After a few years in that activity, he went back to the A.C.M. as weigh master, and later as librarian at the smelter. He was keenly interested in weather statistics and was the city's official government weather observer. He also served as justice of the peace of Deer Lodge county. He was promi-

Frank Kennedy

nent in the Masons and in the Episcopal church. His interest in books probably was one of the reasons he accepted appointment to the library board, a position he filled very capably for 9 years.

Written into the minutes of the board meeting of May 28, 1925, very likely from the pen of E.B. Catlin, is a resolution on the death of Mr. Kennedy:

> On the afternoon of May 2, 1925, after a short illness, Judge Frank Kennedy peacefully passed away. It is fitting at this time that we give expression to our respect and esteem for the colleague who has been lead away from our circle by the hand of death.

We shall long remember Frank Kennedy for his devotion to this institution, his scholarship, his fine appreciation of literary values, his discriminating sense of the needs and requirements of this institution, all of which made him a most valuable member of this board. But above all we shall remember him for his genial nature, his fine character, courtly manner and loveable disposition, that endeared him to all whose privilege it was to know him and call him friend. He lived in this community many years, honored and respected by his fellows; he leaves behind him a record of duty well performed and generous acts kindly bestowed. He set an example of right living that distinguished him as an ideal husband, father and citizen. He attended to the work of his Master most successfully and has passed on to receive the rich reward that awaits him. While we shall miss him and mourn his loss we can but believe that he has entered into a well earned rest safe in God.

Another early-day trustee whose interest in the library was evidenced by terms spanning 25 years was John E. 'Jerry' Clifford. A highly popular man in town, Mr. Clifford was employed in several different capacities by the A.C.M. after his arrival in Anaconda in 1901.

Prior to coming to this city he had a colorful career. He was born in Platte county, Missouri in 1862, and in 1882 graduated from St. Mary's college in Potawatomic county, Kansas. He worked in several clerical positions for the Missouri Pacific Railway before coming to Montana in 1886. He worked for the Missoula Mercantile company for awhile, and then took charge of a large stock of goods for T.J. DeMers bound for Indian country on the Flathead.

In 1888 President Cleveland appointed him postmaster at his store, and the community around it was named 'Clifford' in his honor. He filled that office for two years and also served there as a deputy U.S. marshall. In 1894 Mr. Clifford accompanied the United States commission to Alaska to determine the boundary lines between that territory and Canada.

Upon his return to Montana, he spent several years in

Missoula and in Butte before coming to Anaconda in 1901. In 1908 he was elected recording secretary of the Mill and Smeltermen's union. He was a deputy game warden for four years. He served two terms as a state parole officer. He was active in the Democratic party, being chairman of the state central committee, and holding various offices in the committee in Deer Lodge county.

He served as sponsor for many baseball and other athletic clubs and was manager of the early-day Anaconda Junior Baseball club. Mr. Clifford took an active part in several fraternal organizations, being a member of the Moose, Eagles, and Woodmen of the World. A host of friends, old and young, mourned his death in November 1936 at age 74.

Arthur L. Stone, who was appointed to the board in 1905 and served only two years until he left Anaconda, went on to make his mark on Montana's history in another location. Upon his appointment to the board, he was associate editor of the *Anaconda Standard*. He left that position to become editor of the *Missoulian*, and from there went on to become the first Dean of the School of Journalism at the University of Montana. Under his leadership, the journalism school became one of the top schools in the country. He retired from that position in 1942. To honor its distinguished founder, the journalism school in 1957 inaugurated the Dean Stone Night Dinner and the Dean Stone Visiting Lectures Program.

Mary E. Johnson racked up 18 years as a board member from 1946 to 1964. She was appointed to replace her husband, Oscar A. Johnson, who had served since his appointment in 1940 until his death in 1946. Mrs. Johnson arrived in Anaconda on the train, as an infant, on the day the smelter at Carroll burned down in 1889. She married Oscar Johnson in 1908, at which time he was an auditor for the B.A.& P. railway. She taught school for many years. She was active in the Methodist church, Daughters of the Nile, Eastern Star and American Legion Auxiliary.

Elizabeth Walker Dougherty was another trustee whose service to the library extended to 16 years. She was county superintendent of schools at the time of her appointment in 1946, and she served as board secretary until her resignation in 1962. Prior to becoming county superintendent, Miss Walker was a popular teacher in the Anaconda school system. She married James J. Dougherty in 1948. She died in Yakima, Washington at the home of her daughter on December 11, 1996.

Although Rosealba Laist's term on the board of trustees only lasted for three years, her place in Anaconda's history is deserving of mention. The wife of Frederick Laist, who replaced E.P. Mathewson as general manager of the Anaconda smelter, Rosealba was appointed to the board in 1925, the first woman to serve in that position. The Laists made their home in Anaconda from 1908 until 1929. She was a native of Butte. In 1926, Mrs. Laist was one of the speakers at the State Library convention, which she and Miss Catlin arranged to be held in Anaconda. The text of her address was printed and distributed to the various libraries around the state.

She was also a capable writer, and a book of her adventures on a tour to the continent entitled *Impressions of Europe* was published by the *Anaconda Standard* and became a treasured remembrance to her many friends. The Laists had a beautiful home on Georgetown Lake which they continued to enjoy even after they were sent to New York in 1929 when Frederick was promoted to vice president of metallurgical operations of the Anaconda Copper Mining Company. At the time of their departure, the employees of the Anaconda properties at Anaconda, Great Falls, East Helena and Timber Butte presented the Laists with a painting by C. M. Russell entitled *Squaws Looking for a Camp Site*. Mrs. Laist said she had always wanted a Russell painting, and the gift was "much more than a picture."

The Laists, before they left Anaconda presented the library with a check for $1000 to be used for the purchase of children's books.

The championship for longevity on the library board goes to Helen Wallace, who was appointed by Mayor Ralph Thorson in 1939. Wife of Charles A. Wallace, owner of the Duval-Wallace Hardware store, a long-time Anaconda business, Mrs. Wallace devoted practically a life-time to the library, serving an unbeatable 43 years, 40 years as chairman. She watched 31 other board members come and go during her tenure, which lasted until ill health forced her retirement in 1982. The Wallaces were both

Helen Wallace

active in civic affairs. During her presidency of the American Legion Auxiliary, Mrs. Wallace was instrumental in forming the first session of Girls State. She was elected National Vice President of the Northwestern Division of the Legion Auxiliary. She was president of the Anaconda Women's Club, and her talents as an executive were also appreciated by the Eastern Star and Daughters of the Nile, Deer Lodge County Red Cross and the Board of Deacons of the Presbyterian church.

Mrs. Wallace was an inspiration to another group of women, who served with her on the board from the 1960's to the mid 1980's; Rose McLean, wife of Rodney E. McLean, Natalie Fitzpatrick, a teacher at Anaconda High school, and Agnes Troyer, county superintendent of schools, who provided dedicated leadership for 24, 22 and 21 years respectively. Frances Davis, councilwoman, joined them from 1975 to 1986, and under their careful guidance, during a period of very tight money, the library achieved a fine balance of service to all types of patrons during its busiest years; from small children to teenagers, college students and older adults. To serve all adequately in one basic reading room for 63 hours per week proved a real challenge. During their tenure and with the very able assistance of William Spraycar, who was the city council representative on the board from 1973 to 1975, some much needed basic maintenance was undertaken on the building, which was re-wired, the interior wall drains replaced, a new roof put on, and the building was accepted on the National Register of Historic Places.

In 1933 the city council decided to send an alderman to Library board meetings apparently to serve one year or until replaced. The aldermen are so noted on the following list of trustees.

Board of Trustees, Hearst Free Library

E. P. Mathewson	1904-1916
M. B. Greenwood	1904-1905
G. B. Winston	1904-1905
F. V. Hurley	1904-1907
H. A. Denny	1904-1907
A. L Stone	1905-1907
C.A. Tuttle	1905-1908
C. H. Repath	1907-1909
W. K. Dwyer	1907-1946
J. E. Clifford	1908-1933
E. B Catlin	1908-1933
Warren Jenny	1909-1916
Charles Demond	1916-1923
Frank Kennedy	1916-1925
George C. Jackson	1923-1934
Mrs. Fred Laist	1925-1928

Some Other Board Members of Note

Mrs. W. C. Capron	1927-1930
Mrs. S.S. Rogers	1930
Mrs. E.L. Kunkel	1933-1938
*Angus Eamon	1933-1934
Eldon Larison	1934-1936
*Frank Finnegan	1934-1936
*Dave McIntyre	1936-1938
Maurice Hoyt	1936-1939
*Michael Mee	1938-1939
Jack White	1938-1945
*Leo Jacques	1939-1945
Helen Wallace	1939-1982
Oscar A. Johnson	1940-1946
*Thomas B. Leonard	1945-1946
*Wm. Dumonthier	1946-1947
Elizabeth Walker Dougherty	1946-1962
Mrs. Mary Johnson	1946-1964
Anthony Lubke	1946-1954
*Robert Glynn	1947-1949
*Carl Anderson	1949-1951
*Thomas J. Walsh	1951-1952
*James P. Ryan	1951-1952
*Mario Ungaretti	1952-1953
*Robert McEwan	1953-1957
Leo Kelly	1954-1955
Rev. G. Van Bockern	1955-1959
*Peter Byrne	1957-1959
*Wallace Mehrens	1959-1961
Hollis McCrea	1959-1962
*Fred Frankovich	1962-1963
*Raymond Fleming	1962-1963
Carra Brolin	1962-1965
Rose McLean	1962-1986
Natalie Fitzpatrick	1964-1986
*Harold Hammond	1965-1967
*Loyal Johnson	1964-1965
Bill Yeoman	1965-1968
Agnes Troyer	1965-1986
*Don Gates	1967-1968

*Jack Schulte	1969-1970
*Tom McNelis	1970-1973
*Bill Spraycar	1973-1975
*Frances Davis	1975-1986
Naomi DeLong	1982-1987
Debbie Siders	1986-1988
Mary Jo Oreskovich	1986-1989
JoEllen Drescher	1986-1990
Ellen Lappin	1986-1993
Sandra Conrady	1987-1995
Lianna Schmidt	1988-1995
Bob Ballard	1989-1993
Theresa McCarthy	1990-1995
Betty Wyant	1993-
Paul Beausoleil	1993-
E.L. 'Buzzy' Peterson	1995-
Lorraine Biggs Gallik	1995-
Mary Currie	1995-1996
Marian Geil	1996-

* Aldermen

10 Hitting the Highlights in Library Board Minutes

Reading through the minutes of the board meetings across the years makes it plain that running a public library is not a very exciting pastime. What becomes clear is that with such limited funding, it is usually a real challenge to spread the funds out to get the most use out of them. Purchasing such mundane articles as a typewriter or an adding machine takes on great drama when trying to figure if the item is more sorely needed than a handful of new titles for the fiction collection, or coal for the stoker.

But it is this trivia that makes up not only the life of the library trustee, but also the history of the institution; so if you want to know when the balustrade was removed from the roof, or when the first carpet was installed, read on.

Immediately after the board took over in 1904, they began placing curbing around the library property and beautifying the grounds.

The Women's Literary Club was given permission to use the upstairs reading room for their meetings, as permission for use of a library room for literary purposes had previously been allowed by Mrs. Hearst.

The key words here were *for literary purposes.* The Indenture of 1904 which was the agreement between Phoebe Hearst and the City of Anaconda contained an interesting interlineation of the words, *and for no other purpose* after the words *for a public library,* which was done before the signing, and so noted by the Notary Public to whom Mrs. Hearst took the document. Thus the key phrase in the Indenture reads that *the building would be held in trust for a public library and for no other purpose..*

This point is emphasized in a letter from Fred Clark to Mrs. Winston in January 1901 regarding an entertainment the Women's Club wanted to put on in their meeting room, in which

Mr. Clark, incidentally, referred to the group as the 'Women's Library Club.' He pointed out that he felt the entertainment was undesirable because it would set a precedent, and made it clear that entertainments Mrs. Hearst had in view *were to be given by the library.*

One wonders if the interlineation was made in view of the fact that as early as 1898, the Women's Literary Club had received overtures from the General Federation of Women's Clubs to become affiliated with the Federation and thus change their function from that of a literary group to one with a more social emphasis.

In 1906 the board was occupied with the changeover to an open shelf system of circulation which necessitated re-cataloging the library. Fifty seven trees were purchased from Mr. Greig and planted in the boulevards around the building.

For several years thereafter, business conducted by the board as reflected in the minutes was routine. Gifts were accepted, including many stuffed animals which were displayed in the upstairs reference room. In 1909, a gift of twenty five yellow pine trees from Mr. Call of the Forestry Service, to be set on library grounds, was accepted.

In May, 1911, the About the City column in the *Anaconda Standard* included the following entertaining tidbit: 'While passing by the Hearst Free Library yesterday morning, William Wraith, superintendent of the Washoe Smelter, was met by the Rev. Dr. Carnahan of the Presbyterian church. "Looks as though someone's hen is using the steps of the library for a roost," said Dr. Carnahan. Mr. Wraith left the pavement and walked toward the steps of the building and the bird, which was a full-grown female grouse, took wing and flew in the direction of Washoe Park.'

In 1914 a small ad appeared in the *Anaconda Standard*: 'REWARD: A liberal reward will be paid by the trustees of Hearst Free Library for information leading to the arrest and conviction of the vandals who destroyed the young trees on the grounds of the library on Thursday night, February 12.' There is no mention whether these were Mr. Greig's trees, which were probably the poplars which were planted all over town and in the park about then,) or the yellow pines from Mr. Call. Since there was never any further mention of the pines, we can probably safely assume that they met their demise at this time. The surviving poplars lasted until 1936.

The Women's Club is mentioned again in board minutes in March of 1917 when permission was granted to the club to install a piano, permission to be annulled by the board at their pleasure. The piano was not such a good idea from the library's point of view as in November of 1918, the 'building committee' was instructed to make suitable arrangements 'to eliminate the annoying disturbance that sometimes occurs during the meetings of the Women's Club.' The clatter of sixty pairs of high heeled shoes and the cheerful ring of a piano, often accompanied by the club's 25 voice choir, were not conducive to study in the reading room below; to say nothing of the enticing smell of brewing coffee which permeated the building during meetings and entertainments.

During the years of the First World War, board minutes indicate that the staff of the library were busy collecting books to be sent to army camps, and for the benefit of the troops that were stationed in Anaconda (to protect the smelter) a number of additional newspaper subscriptions were secured. Two large writing tables, added to the furnishings, were well used by the soldiers.

In 1919, new lighting fixtures were installed on the main floor, consisting of attractive bowls for semi-direct lighting of the reading tables, with simple but suitable reflecting shades to illuminate the book shelves.

Into the minutes of April 29, 1919 was read a resolution on the death of Phoebe Hearst, which concluded:

> *Hearst Free Library will always stand as a fitting monument to one whose kind acts will live long after this generation has passed; and its care and maintenance will be considered a sacred trust by our citizens so long as it shall endue to serve its beneficent purpose. To Mrs. Hearst, and now to her memory, the people of Anaconda extend their gratitude and highest esteem.*

Four months after the death of Phoebe Hearst, library board chairman Edwin Catlin stated the substance of a response he had made to a request from the Women's Club for special privileges, which would virtually involve the conversion of the library building into a community center. The two points of the request were: First, the conversion of a part or the whole of the upper floor into a public auditorium for concerts and lectures; Second, the making of a special entrance for the use of members of the Women's Club in connection with their meetings. The response, which was approved by all members of the board, was that while they wholly approved the desire for a suitable community center, this building was not adapted for that, and any plan to convert it to such use would interfere with the proper conduct of the library. As for a special entrance, that was felt quite unnecessary.

The Literary Club had affiliated with the Federated Women's Clubs in May, 1915, so they were really no longer a 'literary club' although the trustees continued to consider them such, even as late as 1948.

It was reported to the board in May of 1920 that mischievous young people were injuring the bound volumes of the *Anaconda Standard* which for a long time had been kept in special cases, and it was decided to move the files downstairs to the magazine room for safety.

Another reference to the Women's Club shows up in the minutes of January 31, 1922, when it was ordered that a letter be sent to the Women's Club emphasizing that none of their exercises should interfere with the quiet that is necessary in a library, and calling their attention to the fact that their use of the building was expected to be only for intellectual and cultural purposes.

As early as 1929, Mr. Dwyer was asked to investigate the possibility of additional funding from designation as a county library, but nothing came of it.

On March 13, 1940, when arriving for work at 5:55 p.m., the assistant, Miss Sliepcevich, smelled smoke in the reading room. Upon investigation, she and Miss Catlin found smoke billowing from the former Ladies Writing Room in the northwest corner of the upstairs. One of the boards appointed by the county was using the room for an office, permission for which was not mentioned in the records of the library, and upon leaving for the day had apparently left something, possibly a cigarette in a wastebasket, which had set the place afire.

The city fire department arrived quickly, and for at least an hour, fought the stubborn blaze which had eaten its way through the floor and was between the floor and the ceiling. The library had to be closed for two weeks for cleaning, painting and repairs. After that experience, the policy of using the upstairs only for library or cultural affairs was more carefully followed.

A long-lived improvement occurred in 1941 when the board authorized installation of the Gaylord Electric Bookcharging system. The simple but effective machine has been a popular one in libraries across the country, and prompted an interesting remembrance to a visitor in the library in January of 1995. A gentleman from Deer Lodge stopped in to look around and remember his youth in Anaconda. He admitted he had not been in the library for thirty years, but still dreamed about it, and had very pleasant memories of time spent in the building when he was a boy. "Every once in awhile when I put a dish on the shelf in my kitchen, it makes a click that reminds me of the sound made by the book charging machine in this library," he reminisced.

The librarian picked up a date card and pushed it in the machine. "That's it!" he exclaimed in amazement. "Is that the same machine?" The librarian laughed and admitted the machine had been changed several times since then, but still operated on the same basic principle, inexpensive and effective for fifty years.

In March of 1943, Miss Catlin arrived at work and found custodian Barney McTigue dead on the floor, apparently from a heart attack. He had been putting out the newspapers when he was stricken.

Mr. Eck, local contractor, inspected the decorative balustrade on the roof in July 1943, and recommended its removal. By October 1944, there was finally enough funds to pay Mr. Semmons of the Anaconda Tin Shop for doing the work.

In 1950 an emergency meeting was held because of the coal shortage. There was only enough coal left to heat the library for a few days, so Mr. Blattner and Mr. Schmidt, the only plumbers in town, were contacted to inquire the cost of converting to gas. The job was given to Mr. Schmidt for $778. It is interesting to note that board approval for converting from coal to natural gas was voted in February 1932.

In October 1962, a contract for a new fence on the east side was let to Mr. Clark and Mr. Pearson for $500.

Also about this time, the board gave approval to the Women's

Club to 'once again occupy the front room on the second floor, as set forth originally in the recorded minutes of August 20, 1904,' with any expenses incurred to be the responsibility of the club. In comparing this information with that in the Women's Club Community Improvement Program report written by Ruth Carmichael in February 1964, we assume it was probably at this time the club installed the kitchen facilities and the restroom in the area that was originally the Ladies Writing Room. They also put up curtains and had the chairs recovered, which made a very pleasant place to hold their meetings.

Meanwhile, the library board, in their long-range plan, were considering the use of the upstairs for expansion of the children's department.

On April 30 to May 1, 1965, the Montana Library Association 52nd Annual Conference was held in Anaconda, chaired by Librarian Natalie Sliepcevich, who had just completed her term as president of the state association. Hosting the conference was a major undertaking for a library with a staff of two, and the meeting facilities of the community were taxed to capacity with the sizeable group of librarians, trustees and vendors who descended upon the town for the event.

An informal group of library friends, including the Women's Club and the Soroptimists, among others, rallied around and worked for a year making necessary arrangements for the conference which was centered at the Montana Hotel, with exhibits held in the Elks Club, much to the delight of the exhibitors. Book salesmen for twenty years afterward recalled fondly the conference held in Anaconda.

The speaker at the opening luncheon was Mrs. Vonnie Eastham of Chico, California, whose subject was 'Phoebe Hearst, Philanthropist.' Mrs. Eastham was considered one of the foremost authorities at the time on Phoebe Hearst, having researched the lady's life for several years for a biography. Unfortunately she passed away before the book could be published, and it was many years before Judith Robinson finally came up with a definitive biography on Mrs. Hearst. Mrs. Eastham's talk was a delight to conference attendees who then doubly appreciated their visit to the library for a coffee hour hosted by the Anaconda Women's Club.

A new lighting system was installed later that year in the main floor reading room by Marcotte Electric, paid for by a grant from the Hearst Foundation arranged by Librarian Natalie Sliepcevich.

During the last two years of the 1960's, the oak panels on the interior entry doors were replaced with glass, which made the vestibules more visible from the librarian's desk, thus eliminating much mischief in the formerly secluded areas. Also, carpet was installed for the first time in the main reading room, as the hardwood floors had been sanded to the point where they were wearing thin. Scraping chairs, dropping pencils and thundering footsteps became a distraction of the past.

The highlight of 1969 was also one of the highlights of the history of the library; the visit of William Randolph Hearst, grandson of Phoebe and George, which is covered more fully in chapter 12.

As mentioned earlier in this account, George and Phoebe had only one child, William Randolph. Will and his wife Millicent, in turn, had five sons, George, John, William, and twins, Randolph and David. As children, the boys spent many happy hours with their grandmother at her home in Pleasanton. At the time of his visit to Anaconda, William was publisher of the *San Francisco Chronicle*, and chairman of the board of the Hearst Corporation. The board minutes record that at the July 28 meeting, the secretary was instructed to write a letter to Mr. Hearst expressing their appreciation for his visit to the library. In September, receipt of a letter from him to the board expressed his thanks for their hospitality.

In 1973 the Library was nominated to the National Register of Historic Places, and celebrated its Diamond Jubilee with an Open House and Reception.

In late 1974, Bill Spraycar, the city representative to the board of trustees, reported that there was money available for restoration of historic buildings. Since the roof had developed severe leaks due to heavy snowfall, the Community Development Office was contacted to see if funding was available for such repair. Subsequently, some very essential major repair work was completed on the building, including a new roof, replacement of interior wall drains, and cleaning exterior brick. Three additional stacks were added to the adult section, fitted with handmade canopies to make them look like the originals.

Natalie Sliepcevich introduces William R. Hearst, Jr. to library patrons, Steve and Tom Mullen. Austin Hearst at the right. 1969.

In June of 1975, the Anaconda Eagles Auxiliary made the first of many donations to the library earmarked for purchase of Large Type books. The much appreciated gift provided the nucleus for the library's Large Type book collection.

In spring of 1977, consolidation of city and county government into Anaconda-Deer Lodge County finally involved the county in library funding.

Since 1963's long-range plan, the board had considered the possibility of moving the children's department upstairs, thus freeing up more space in the main reading room. With that in mind, when Community Development Office asked for plans for continuing the improvement of the upstairs in 1977, the Women's Club was asked to find other quarters. A fire escape was installed, through the efforts of the Anaconda Company. Extensive rewiring, removal of the partition between the two large reference rooms and general cleanup were accomplished. Plans for a complete juvenile reading and study area were laid out.

Carol Goodger-Hill of Bozeman Public Library attended a special meeting to acquaint trustees with services to be provided by

Margaret Durkin and Eleanor Ivankovich inspect the art exhibit. 75th Anniversary Celebration, 1973

the recently organized Broad Valleys Federation of Libraries, including interlibrary loans, large print books, on-line computer research, etc. A contract with them was signed.

In December 1979, the county cut the library budget by $10,000. All phases of operation were re-examined to find where a bare-bones budget could be even further cut.

On September 26, 1980, it was announced that all the upstairs work had been completed, and the area was ready for furnishing. On September 29, the smelter closed, and threw all county funding into chaos. Plans for moving the children's section were cancelled.

1983 was highlighted by the purchase of two Texas Instruments computers for patron use in the library. The move was watched closely by other libraries in the Broad Valleys Federation, which were considering the purchase of computers for public use. Classes conducted at the library were well attended.

In 1985, another nice grant secured from the Hearst Foundation by Librarian Sliepcevich resulted in several more improvements including new Venetian blinds throughout the building, a larger card catalog, a new photocopy machine and a much needed microfilm reader-printer.

In September 1989 the County commissioners removed the library from the General Fund, stating there was not enough tax money coming in to cover the requested budget. The library was named Repository for Superfund Documents. Massive amounts of documentation on Superfund remedial cleanup of industrial waste sites were being generated.

At the general election of 1990, 71.6% of the registered voters were in favor of increasing millage for operation of the library, and a Special Library Fund was created.

Throughout 1993 serious consideration was given to the requirements of the Americans with Disabilities Act. (ADA) Handicapped access had been discussed for 30 years, but the ADA made action imperative. New carpet was installed, and plans were revived briefly for putting the children's department upstairs.

With the deadline for compliance with ADA rapidly approaching, many public meetings were held and the discussions finally culminated in installation of a ramp and automatic door on the Main street entrance, and a compromise rest room on the main floor which eliminated the need of tearing up all three floors of the building for an elevator. In August 1996 the ramp was formally dedicated to the memory of Catherine Spellman, whose generous bequest to the library which had provided her so much reading pleasure during her lifetime, made it possible.

In 1997, the library was one of the winners of a free Internet hookup from Broad Valleys Federation, so the Jr. Women's Club computer for children and another for adult use were installed in the reading room, and immediately became very busy. The board accepted a gift from retired teacher and school administrator, Mary Dolan, for an adult computer center to be installed at the library to encourage older Anacondans to become computer literate.

Another long-range plan adopted by the board is expected to lead to automation of the library circulation system.

The board also accepted a proposal from Mike Kovacich, local clock builder, to install a large ornate clock on the front lawn, near the corner of Main and Fourth streets, to commemorate the Library's Centennial Celebration. The timepiece is to be dedicated to the memory of Phoebe Apperson Hearst.

11 Treasures Within the Library

The blankness of the walls is pleasantly broken by pictures of more than ordinary interest and art value. There are portraits of Senator Hearst and Mrs. Hearst, and a number of oils, engravings, and photogravures. In one corner is a well-executed bust of Senator Hearst in marble. A burntwood portrait of Agassiz is worthy of particular notice. (On the second floor) every wall space has its engraving, pastel, photogravure or oil, forming a well selected nucleus for an art gallery." Thus does the *Anaconda Standard* of June 12, l898, introduce its readers to the art collection of the newly opened Hearst Free Library in Anaconda.

The very fact that most of these original art works still grace the walls of the library was a major factor in the library's being named to the National Register in 1973, and they remain a constant and largely unrecognized treasure within the community.

Three of the paintings originally chosen by Mrs. Hearst for display in the library were returned to her at her request, and replaced by her with other paintings. In 1905, a letter was received from Edward Clark on behalf of Mrs. Hearst, asking that two paintings be expressed to her at Pleasanton, California. The two were 'Discovery of San Francisco Bay' by William Keith, and 'An Old Whaling Ship.' A second Keith painting referred to in board minutes as 'A Grove of Oak Trees' was returned to Mrs. Hearst at her request in 1915.

The artist, William Keith, was born in Aberdeenshire, Scotland, on November 21, 1838. He was a prolific painter, and by the turn of the century, was California's best known landscapist. His studio was near the grove of live oaks on the Berkeley campus, and the oaks figured in many of his canvases. 'Discovery of San Francisco Bay' serves as the frontispiece in a

View of Cairo: oil painting by Carl Oscar Borg

book called 'California, Romantic and Resourceful' by John F. Davis, published by A.M. Robertson of San Francisco in 1914.

Mrs. Hearst owned at least two Keith oak tree paintings, so the one returned to her in 1915 could have been either 'Tapestry Oaks' or 'Moonrise Among the Oaks.' There was an article in the Chicago Tribune of July 24, 1893 about the latter picture which stated: "The last picture painted by Mr. Keith before setting his face to the East created quite a sensation in San Francisco and was purchased by Mrs. Hearst, widow of the late Senator Hearst. Its title was 'Moonrise Among the Oaks,' and its weird character amply justifies Mr. Keith's remark about it, that he was so lost to ordinary surroundings during the time he was painting it that he could not remember his progress upon it, step by step, as he usually could after a work was done—that he sometimes found it difficult to believe that he really painted it."

Over 2,000 of Keith's paintings, sketches and studies were

Northwest Wind: oil painting by Richard Langtry Partington

lost in the San Francisco earthquake and fire of 1906. Although 70 years old at the time, he set out to reproduce as many of those as possible. Keith died in Berkeley in 1911. There are several good books on his life and art works available.

The paintings which were chosen by Mrs. Hearst to replace the Keiths were 'View of Cairo' by Carl Oscar Borg, and 'Northwest Wind' by R. L. Partington. In a letter written to Warren Jenny, secretary to the board of the library on April 7, 1915, Mrs. Hearst explained that she had not yet found a suitable marine view to replace the Keith painting. "A good many have been considered," she wrote, "some of which were too small, and others unsatisfactory in different ways; but I do not doubt that eventually I shall find one which will be as acceptable to the Board and to the people of Anaconda as the painting for which it is substituted."

"Meantime," the letter continued, "I have had framed and sent to you an interesting scene of Cairo, by a clever Swedish artist, Carl Oscar Borg, who, though only thirty-three or four years old, has had a good many successful pictures in European exhibitions. Hoping this Oriental scene will please those who visit the Library, I am Yours Very Truly, Phoebe A. Hearst."

Shortly thereafter, on June 26, 1915, Mrs. Hearst wrote again to explain the arrival of a second Borg painting, which

Withered Woman: etching by Hubert Herkomer

was a gift to the library from the artist. "This is by no means a substitute for the marine view I promised to send you, and for which I shall have to ask you to wait until after the close of the Panama-Pacific International Exposition in San Francisco. I have found nothing outside of the Exposition that seemed suitable and satisfactory to me, but there are several fine views on the walls of the Fine Arts building which will be for sale when the Exposition is over, and I will then make a selection of one for the library."

Later, on March 8, 1916, Mrs. Hearst reported to Miss Thomson that she had been unable to find a view at the

Exposition. She had visited the studio of 'one of our best marine artists' in New York, however, hoping to be able to purchase directly from the artist rather than through a dealer. He had only small canvasses, she wrote, but "promised that as soon as he had finished a good sized picture or two, he would let me know."

Whether this letter refers to Richard Langtry Partington, the creator of 'Northwest Wind,' is unknown, but that is the painting which was received at the library in November, 1916, as the long-awaited replacement for Keith's 'Discovery of San Francisco Bay.' Partington seems to be remembered primarily as a portrait painter. Born in Stockport, England, on December 7, 1868, he studied under his father, J. H. Partington, a noted English artist, also with Hubert Herkomer, and at the Beaux Arts Institute in Antwerp. People from all over the world sat for portraits at his studio, according to American Art Annals. He was a member of the San Francisco Art Association, the Philadelphia Art Alliance, and other organizations in this country and in England. Partington died in Philadelphia on June 5, 1929.

As an interesting coincidence, there is a Hubert Herkomer etching in the library's collection, it was upstairs for many years, but came out of hiding in 1973 to be hung in the librarian's office, along with two lovely etchings by L. E. Eldred, and one by Peir Vernon. It is believed they were in the Ladies Writing Room, maybe transferred from the old library.

Carl Oscar Borg had attracted the attention of Phoebe Hearst when he first arrived in California as a young man in his 20's. As with many of the young people in whom she took an interest, Mrs. Hearst provided the opportunity for Borg to pursue his studies in art by sending him to Europe for five years of intensive study with master painters. Upon his return to California he embarked upon a remarkable career as a painter of the Southwest. He became a close friend of Ed Borein, who specialized in cattle, horses and cowboy life; but Borg went beyond these subjects and also painted Indian ceremonials and landscapes. The selection of Borg's painting 'LeChateau Gaillard ' (the ruined castle of Richard the Lion Hearted in LesAndelys) to be exhibited at the Panama Pacific

Senator George Hearst: oil painting by Georgina Campbell

Exposition showed his qualifications as an international artist, in the years when Western art had become a subject of national interest in this country.

He lived with the Hopi and Navajo for awhile, and was able to present their ceremonials and way of life with great feeling and integrity. By the time he died in 1947, he had become one of California's best known artists.

The portrait of Senator George Hearst which dominates the main reading room of the library was painted by Georgina Campbell, apparently during the Washington, D. C. years. The artist was born in 1861 in New Orleans into a wealthy and socially prominent family. She studied art for several years in Paris, and at the World's Fair in 1883. Miss Campbell had always painted portraits 'for fun' until after the death of her father, she decided to go into it seriously. She moved to New York, where she maintained a studio on fashionable Madison Avenue. She painted many prominent people besides Senator Hearst, including senators Stewart, Dolph, and Field; General Grant, and four portraits for the family of Senator Stanford. When someone suggested she try her hand at miniatures which were coming back into vogue, she did so, with great success. James Morris, a celebrated English collector, considered her to be one of the finest painters of the period. Her portraits are in many cities in the United States, as well as abroad. She died in 1931. The frame on the Campbell portrait bears the mark of Henry Leidel Artists Materials of New York.

The marble bust of Senator Hearst which is over the fireplace was created by James Paxton Voorhees. The bust was for many years on a stand in the corner, and was not placed in the niche provided for it until 1927. Voorhees was born in Covington, Indiana on October 1, 1855, and was educated in Terre Haute, and at Georgetown College in Washington, D. C. He went into newspaper work at age 16, and also read law in the office of his father. He followed a theatrical profession for a time, and then became private secretary to his father, Daniel W. Voorhees, when he became a senator.

Two of Voorhees' portrait busts are on exhibit in Statuary Hall at the U. S. Capitol, those of the Kentuckians, Richard M. Johnson, and J. C. Breckenridge. He also did one of his father, Daniel W. Voorhees, and among others, did Jefferson and Napoleon for the St. Louis Exposition. Somewhere along the way, he also found time to publish several novels.

The Library's 75th anniversary celebration in 1973 featured a display of five fine Peter Toft watercolors, which may have been among the pictures moved from the old library at Third and Cherry, for they were in the Ladies Reading Room at the time of the opening. One of the pictures called 'View from the Balcony of Cliff House' is inscribed "To Mrs. P.E.Hearst from one of her many friends—Christmas 1864."

The Montana State Historical Society owns a number of

Storks Nesting: watercolor by Peter Toft

Toft paintings, some of which were donated by Senator W.A. Clark. The Montana Post, November 24, 1866, said, "Mr. Toftt,[sic] who has traveled through Washington, Oregon and Montana, has painted some of the most sublime and picturesque objects of nature that he witnessed in these sections. An examination of his portfolio will satisfy all that he is an artist of exquisite taste."

The Helena Daily Herald, March 19, 1870, refers to him as "an artist of considerable skill and genius, who visited Montana during the summer of 1868, while making a tour

Westminister Abbey: watercolor by Peter Toft

through the Pacific states and territories..."

Toft is featured in such company as Remington, Russell, Catlin, Bodmer, Moran and others in a book by Larry Curry entitled 'The American West.'

The pictures in the collection of the Hearst Free Library, besides the afore mentioned View from the Balcony of Cliff House (which was later destroyed in the 1906 earthquake) include: The Fortress of San Juan d'Ulua, Vera Cruz, Mexico, May 1 1889; The Coast of Sark, Channel Islands, not dated;

Storks Nesting, not dated; and Poets Corner, Westminster Abbey, May 1879.

Peter Peterson Toft was born in Denmark and at age 17, went to sea on a whaling ship. He later joined a North American ship-of-war. While touring Montana in 1866, he was injured in a fall from his horse, and while recuperating, determined to become a professional painter. He had painted since childhood, and soon built up an international reputation. He traveled extensively over North and South America, Asia and North Africa, and eventually settled in London. He had a light and graceful touch and his odd, unusual subjects appealed to the public. His composition and color work were pleasing in their simplicity. He was modest and unassuming, did not have much education, but his skill was that of a technician. He was considered a master painter. He died in London in 1901.

Two other fine oil paintings are in the collection. At the head of the stairs on the second floor landing is a large painting of the donkey which was responsible for the discovery of the Bunker Hill mine in Idaho. The artist was Mathilda Lotz, who was born in Tennessee in 1861.

Often compared to Rosa Bonheur because of her depictions of animals, Lotz worked mostly in pastels and oils, painting many landscapes and scenes of everyday life. She studied with J. Williams of San Francisco, and with F.J. Barrias in Paris. She resided in California for a large part of her life, but traveled extensively in Europe, the Middle East, the Orient and North Africa. Her work was exhibited in America, Paris, London, Austria, Hungary and Germany. Her marriage to the painter F. Blastovic took her to Hungary, and it was there that she died in 1923.

The subject of the Lotz painting is an interesting story in itself. According to Anne and Si Frazier, foreign correspondents for *Lapidary Journal*, who visited the library in the summer of 1994, the placid looking jackass of the painting was the property of Noah Kellogg, Idaho prospector, who had received the animal as part of his 'grubstake' from two gentlemen who wanted to get rid of the beast because its insistent braying disturbed the whole mining camp of Murray. While on a prospecting trip, the jack slipped his tether during the night, and Kellogg was chagrined to find himself afoot and alone when he awakened in the morning. He soon heard the animal braying, however, and climbing the mountain behind his camp, finally found his wandering companion with his feet on a marvelous vein of galena, "with one eye cocked" on the outcropping on which he stood, and his ears pointing across the valley to another outcropping on the vein which became the famous Bunker Hill and Sullivan mine.

Kellogg, Idaho, of course, is named after Noah Kellogg, and his jackass was quite a local hero for a time, as Kellogg loved to tell the story of how he made his strike. The animal continued to serenade the camp with his distinctive braying, however, and one day a couple disgruntled miners loaded him with dynamite, lit a long fuse, and ran him out of camp. The resulting blast permitted the community its first uninterrupted night's sleep for some time.

The other painting to be found in the upstairs hallway of the library next to the Lotz and the Borg marine, is a herd of cattle in a serene rural setting. The artist is Alfred Elias, a British artist, who was almost exclusively known for his renderings of animals; cows, sheep and horses, in either English or French landscapes. He exhibited widely in England, at the London Royal Academy from 1885 onward, and beginning in 1882, he regularly showed at the Paris Salon. Examples of his work were included in the Paris International Exhibition of 1889. His wife Emily was also a painter.

Among the fine photographs on the walls of the library since the time of the grand opening is a collection of architectural subjects done by Adolphe Braun (1811-1877) Braun was an important architectural photographer, well regarded at the time for his 'instantaneous' views, notably of the streets of Paris, and of the mountains of Switzerland, according to the Collector's Guide to Photographs, published by Ballantine in 1979. The library's collection of Braun photographs numbers fifteen architectural subjects, and the Venus de Milo.

The Braun photos were received from W.K. Vickery Pictures and Framing of San Francisco, in early May, 1898, with the following letter:

The Librarian
Hearst Free Library
Anaconda, Montana

My dear Sir,

At Mrs. Hearst's request I ship a case containing pictures intended for the walls of the Hearst Free library. The list is sent herewith and the B/L. The freight is prepaid. Another case will follow in a week or so. If these cases do not reach you by or on the 20th please advise me by wire at my expense.

Going by freight, I have taken the precaution to paste strips of paper on the glass to prevent vibration and breakage. Do not be disappointed at your first view of them, for these strips are not beautiful. Please have some boy with hot cloths remove those strips and polish up the glass, and kindly warn him against letting the water touch the frames. I am sorry to give you this trouble and would not if it were avoidable. If not too much trouble may I ask that you let me know if they arrive safely and also have any glasses, if they are broken, replaced and charged to me.

There is not a city in the land but would be glad to have a library furnished with such a splendid collection of pictures. May I wish you personally many years of enjoyment of them.

The list of pictures in this first shipment include: Framed portraits of Agassiz, Benjamin Franklin, O.W. Holmes, Shakespeare, Thomas Jefferson, Alexander Hamilton, Lincoln, George Washington, Martha Washington, George Washington by Marshall, Robert Burns. 5 Braun photographs, architectural subjects Braun Venus de Milo U.S. Frigate Constitution

A portrait of Marshall and ten more Braun photographs, architectural subjects, are to follow.

Yours truly, W.K. Vickery

A second letter from Mr. Vickery dated May 11, 1898 explained that eleven more pictures were being sent by freight on the 14th, as instructed by Mrs. Hearst. He explained that five of the pictures were not to be had in America and had to be ordered from abroad, so sample copies were being sent to temporarily occupy the frames. The copies were to be replaced at his expense upon arrival of the pictures.

The list attached to this letter included:
1. Sphinx and pyramids
2. The Nile
3. Temple of Philae
4. Island of Philae
5. Temple of Karnak
6. Acropolis
7. Temple of Jupiter
8. Carytid Porch of the Erechtheum
9. St. Mark's, Venice
10. Certosa of Pavia
11. Portrait of Marshall

Numbers 4,5,6,7 and 10 were temporary only, owing to the necessity importing from Europe, but were to be substituted by the proper prints as soon as received. As to whether the five pictures were ever replaced, there is no evidence one way or other in library files.

The portrait of Louis Agassiz sent by Mr. Vickery is worthy of particular note, it is a burnt wood portrait very finely done, and marked merely HB 1892 in the lower left hand corner.

The rest of the portraits were, at the time of this writing, hanging in the large room upstairs.

Another set of fine photographs are on the walls of the Gentlemen's Writing Room in the Northeast corner upstairs. They are by William Henry Jackson. According to Richard Blodgett's Collectors Guide to Photographs, William Henry Jackson (1842-1942,) was one of the most colorful and beloved American photographers of the 19th century. Jackson Lake and the city of Jackson, Wyoming, and Jackson Butte in Colorado are named after him. Blodgett tells us that one of Jackson's hallmarks "is the contrast of near and far objects. One of his most significant contributions to American history is his pivotal role in the establishment of Yellowstone as the nation's first national park."

The fact that the five photos just fit the spaces in the room, they are of Yosemite, and they were framed by Morris and

Kennedy Fine Arts of San Francisco, lead this writer to believe they also were chosen by Mrs. Hearst, possibly for that particular room, or at least for the old library, as no mention of them is in the minutes of board meetings as were acquisitions after 1904. The views are marked No. 1347, Glacier Point, Yosemite; No. 1331 The Bridal Veil, Yosemite; No. 1338 The North Dome, Royal Arches and Washington Column; No. 1442 Moss Brae Falls Near Mt. Shasta, and one untitled waterfall in a painted frame.

Jackson is referred to on many occasions in the Montana Magazine of History. When he died in June 1942 he was three months beyond his 99th birthday.

An item of great interest in the minutes and newspapers of September 1912 involves the gift of the statue of *Laocoon and the Sea Serpents* from the High School class of 1912 to the library. The class had hoped to present to the High School, as a remembrance of their class, a replica of the Victory of Samothrace. For one reason or another, the Laocoon was the statuary that was received, and the board of education did not feel the piece was suitable for display in the school. The class therefore offered it to the library.

"There is no reason why the high school students should not present works of art to the library where more people will see them than ever would at the school, and where the artistic value of this statue will be more fully appreciated. We will see it there after we have ceased to visit the school," wrote the class secretary. "We feel very proud to be able to give the people of our city the opportunity of seeing a great piece of sculpture and we hope they will be as glad to accept it as we are to give."

In their letter of acceptance, the Board of Trustees wrote: "That the people of Anaconda will appreciate the happy and convenient opportunity of viewing and possessing such a splendid piece of statuary we feel confident. Let us also assure you that the magnificent cast of the renowned Laocoon group will furnish a stimulus to the artistic taste of this community and remain an enduring memorial of the generosity of the Class of 1912, AHS, We remain thankfully yours, E. P, Mathewson, President, Board of Trustees; Warren Jenny, Secretary.

The students were right in assuming more people would see the statue at the library. Through the years it is one of the art works most often mentioned by former Anacondans who return to visit. A plaster replica of one of the most famous of Greek sculptures, the group represents Laocoon, a priest of Apollo, and his two sons in the clutches of the sea serpents sent by Poseidon on behalf of the Greeks besieging Troy as told in Vergil's Aeneid. Laocoon, in warning the Trojans not to accept the gift of the wooden horse, incurred the wrath of Poseidon. After the sea serpents had silenced the priest and his sons, and the Greeks pretended to sail away, the Trojans moved the wooden horse inside the city walls. In the dark of night the soldiers hidden within the horse came out and unlocked the city gates, allowing the Greek army to swarm in and take the city, thus ending the siege of Troy. The subject was a popular one among Greek sculptors, and the marble original of this particular Laocoon group is in the Vatican at Rome, and is believed to have been created by Agesander, Polydorus and Athenodorus about A.D. 100. The pedestal was provided by William Law and Frank Tucker, local businessmen.

The other art treasure most frequently remembered and inquired about by former patrons is the Audubon's Bird book which for many years was in a glass case by the Main street door. The 1860 Bien edition of Birds of America was entered into the reference department of the library on June 7, 1898, a gift from Fred Clark. The original owner of the book lived in San Francisco.

In 1858 James Woodhouse Audubon joined with Julius Bien, a German immigrant lithographer, in an attempt to reproduce Audubon's father's famous 1827 double-elephant folio bird illustrations by means of the chromolithographic process. The project was intended to include all 435 of the original plates reproduced at full size on double-elephant paper, with the intended sale price of $500, about a half of what the original had cost 20 years earlier.

Bien brought with him from Germany some of the most sophisticated knowledge about printing to be found in America. From a tiny print shop in New York City he built an extremely successful business, which at the time of his death in 1909 employed 200 persons. He received many awards for excellence in producing fine maps. There was a lot of color work produced at the time that was tastelessly done, but the Bien edition of Audubon's Birds of America is regarded as a technical masterpiece of chromolithography.

The plan to reproduce the original plates required artistry, technical daring, and sound financial backing. Unfortunately, the last was the most difficult, and the project was never completed. Probably the death of James Woodhouse Audubon in 1862 pretty well scuttled the project, as the Audubon family finances were already low, and his mother, the widow of John James Audubon, had to sell many of her husband's original art works, just to make ends meet.

It is believed that about 150 plates were actually printed. Critics point out that the work was never finished, that the prints are 'inferior to the original edition,' and emphasize the use of low-quality paper; but in retrospect, it is admitted by many experts that Bien's contributions to American chromolithography are undeniably important and that he put the craft on a solid technical and artistic foundation. Furthermore, his Audubon work was an early milestone in the color revolution in American printing.

The library's volume of the prints probably was on a table in the upstairs reference room, where it could be flipped through at leisure. The plates were 27 x 40 inches, so would have been fairly cumbersome to handle. In the board minutes of February 26, 1918, it was reported that the book was in seriously dilapidated condition, and it was recommended that it should be put away until attention could be given to its repair, and proper display could be arranged. Not until June 1934 is it mentioned again, at which time Mr. McComb, a carpenter, was engaged to build a case for it, for which he was paid $27.50.

The book remained a popular exhibit until 1989 at which time the board of trustees sent it to the state historical society for protective storage in its atmosphere-controlled vault. It remained there until May of 1996 when it was returned to the library and placed back in the case built for it by Mr. McComb back in 1934.

Miscellaneous works rounding out the picture collection include a small oil painting called "Falstaff" signed AB '77.

E.P. Mathewson was the donor of a lithographic print of the Washoe Reduction Works which was given to the library in 1909, having hung in the office of the Old Works for several years.

A pen and ink detail of the columns on the Fourth street entrance was featured on the cover of the *PNLA Quarterly* spring issue in 1976. The original was donated to the library by the artist, Ruth Eckstein of Grants Pass, Oregon.

Two large 'primitive' prints of children, one boy, one girl, artists unknown, were donated by the Anaconda Kiwanis Club in 1990 for the children's section.

Five photographic reproductions of renaissance portraits complete the collection, a reproduction of an oil painting of a "Man in a Red Coat" in an ornate gold frame being the most impressive of these. It, too, was brought down from upstairs in the 1970's to hang in the main reading room. The four others are sepia prints of portraits by European masters of the same era (1510-1530) more simply framed in narrow wood frames. A descriptive article dated 1909 indicates these were probably part of the original collection brought from the old library on Cherry street.

As early as 1895 when Jack Martin killed the beautiful white swan on Lost Creek and gave it to Richard deB. Smith for display, an interesting assortment of items have found their way to the library, and were at first displayed in the upstairs reference room, where old timers especially, remember the collection of stuffed animals, the rock display and the stereoscope pictures.

The fire chief suggested getting rid of the stuffed animals in the 1960's; some of them, that hadn't been 'stuck with a spear until their insides ran out' were refurbished and displayed for awhile at the Copper Village Museum when it was in its first location at the old LDS church on Eighth street.

The rock collection was reorganized for display in 1990 by volunteer Kalmar Stevenson. During the heyday of the Anaconda Company's esteemed Research Department before it was moved to Tucson, a fine display of local minerals was arranged by Lazlo Dudas in a special case in the main reading room, where it was much appreciated by visitors. Those specimens have been absorbed into the collection upstairs. Some of the salvageable smaller miscellaneous items are in the display case on the west wall of the main reading room.

The Robert Lennington Camp, No. 6, United Spanish War Veterans of Anaconda presented an interesting relic for display, a wooden drill from the battleship *Maine*, which was salvaged from the wreck after having laid at the bottom of Havana Harbor. The drill is two feet six inches long and was used in cleaning the guns. The sinking of the *Maine* in Havana Harbor on February 18, 1898, helped spark the Spanish-American war. The battleship had been sent to Havana in January, 1898 'to protect American citizens and property in case of riots.' On February 15, it blew up, killing about 260 crew members. The U.S accused Spain, as Havana was a Spanish port, but Spain claimed it was an internal explosion. "Remember the *Maine*" became a popular sentiment in favor of war against Spain.

American interest in annexing Cuba had existed since the 1860's. Spain had controlled Cuba since Columbus discovered it in 1492, but a series of revolutions through the 1800's convinced many Americans that it would be politically expedient to acquire Cuba. In 1895 acute economic depression there prompted the American press, including newspapers controlled by William Randolph Hearst to print sensational reports of intolerable conditions in Cuba and agitate for American intervention. In 1897 Spain granted Cuba limited self-government, but the rebels continued to fight for independence and the sinking of the *Maine* prompted the U.S. to declare that a state of war existed with Spain.

The Spanish-American War lasted from April to August of 1898, and the newspapers reporting the opening of the Hearst Free Library are also full of war news from Cuba. Today, many historians believe the explosion that sank the *Maine* probably was internal, and not caused by a Spanish mine at all. Spain gave up all claim to Cuba as a result of the war, and the United States won Guam, Puerto Rico and the Philippine islands, and stepped for the first time into the role of a world power.

Nicely displayed in a glass case, the *Maine* relic has survived much longer than the silk banners of Companies K and M, Montana Volunteers, the Anaconda contingent of which trained up Sheep Gulch and went off to fight in the war. Casualties of the Montana Volunteers were very high. The banners have crumbled away to shreds.

The ship model which has delighted so many visitors through the years was created by Knute Miller in 1918, and is a replica of The Liberty, a World War I hospital ship.

The grandfather clock was purchased from Keppler Jewelry of Anaconda in 1910 for $50.

12 The Librarians

Not much information could be found about RICHARD DEB. SMITH who served as the first librarian appointed by Phoebe Hearst. In a letter to Mrs. Helen Hensley of Anaconda dated January 8, 1895, Mrs. Hearst expressed confidence that Richard deB. Smith would be competent and satisfactory in the position (as librarian) and hoped that his acceptance of the offer to fill the position would not occasion any loss to him or deprive him of more remunerative employment.

Several letters from Mr. Smith to Mrs. Hearst are in the collection of the Bancroft Library in Berkeley, California, which refer to routine library business, such as a request to have magazines bound at the Standard Publishing Company, and other reports of activities. In one he suggests that 'Mr. Babbit can more fully explain to you the workings of the library than I could in writing'... dated November 1, 1895.

In another letter dated December 2, 1895 he encloses the monthly report and a 'clipping from the Sunday paper showing how fully people are appreciating the library.' Also in the Bancroft files is his letter of resignation dated December 19. 1895.

In the Hearst Free Library files is a letter from Phoebe Hearst to Fred Clark regarding final settlement with Mr. Smith and suggesting that in evidence of her good will and in view of his faithful service, he be given an extra half month's salary with his final check.

After a brief trip East, following his resignation from the library, Mr. Smith returned to Anaconda and was listed in the 1896 directory as being associated with Thomas F. Mahoney in the Real Estate and General Insurance business at 209 Main. There is no listing in the city directory for him after 1909.

Fred Clark

Fred Clark, as previously mentioned, was a second cousin of the Hearsts, and a trusted family friend. Born in Franklin county, Missouri on January 18, 1860, Fred was the son of Austin Whitmire Clark and his wife Angela Whitley. He married Margaret Johnson of Washington county, Missouri on October 18, 1882.

In 1892 after the death of her husband George, Phoebe was looking for help in managing her affairs. She knew she could trust 'the Clark boys' who were in Fresno, running a grocery store started by their father Austin. Two brothers of Austin had accompanied George Hearst to California on his first trip in 1850; Austin apparently followed later.

Fred's older brother, Edward Hardy Clark was put in charge of the San Francisco office and ranches and eventually became president of the Homestake Mining Company.

Fred was sent to Anaconda to oversee the establishment of the library. He and his family lived at 602 Locust, where a son, Austin William, was born on March 25, 1895, joining a brother Albert, and sisters Jessie and Mildred.

Fred made the Anaconda news on April 20, 1896, when the Standard reported: 'Fred Clark, librarian of the Hearst Free Library, is suffering from a very sore head. He was splitting wood in the back yard, and did not see the clothesline overhead, swung the axe and it caught thereon, fell and struck him in the forehead. Dr. Spellman was summoned and sewed up the gash. It was very unfortunate, but might have been worse.'

Upon the resignation of Richard deB. Smith, Fred assumed the duties of head librarian, and served in that capacity until August 1, 1896, when he was sent to Lead to visit Mrs. Hearst's library there. Miss Isabel Tracy, who had been his assistant, was put in charge, assisted by Miss Anne Douglas.

Fred and Maggie and their family returned to California, where they subsequently lived for many years in Berkeley. Fred continued as Mrs. Hearst's Western agent, and was instrumental in planning the building of the library at Fourth and Main streets. Another daughter was born after they left Anaconda. In about 1899, Fred was named secretary and a director of the Homestake Mining company, a position he held for 25 years.

After Phoebe's death in 1919 Fred was the Western manager for the Hearst estate, and was secretary for the Examiner Publishing Company. The last few years of his life were spent in San Francisco. He died suddenly on December 22, 1923 of a stroke after a Christmas shopping tour. He was 63.

An interesting letter from Fred Clark to Mrs. G. B. Winston, dated January 25, 1901, is in the files of the Bancroft Library in Berkeley. Apparently Mrs. Winston had approached Mr. Clark for permission for the Women's Literary Club to sponsor some sort of an entertainment in the library. Fred stated he had forwarded the letter to Mrs. Hearst in Washington for a reply, but he felt personally it was not in the best interests of the library for any sort of entertainment which would cost the public anything to attend. 'When in Anaconda, Mrs. Hearst visited your Woman's Library [sic] Club, and spoke very highly of it,' he wrote, 'and by letting them have a room at certain times for their exclusive use, the club was being encouraged in every way possible. ' Fred pointed out that should Mrs. Hearst consent to the club giving an entertainment there, naturally churches and societies generally would want the same accommodation. *'The entertainments Mrs. Hearst had in view either literary or musical, were intended to be given by the library,'* he told her.

Isabel Tracy

Miss Isabel Tracy was hired as assistant librarian in 1896, and promoted to head librarian in 1897. She was well thought of in the community and had a lot of friends who read with interest in the June 29, 1897 *Anaconda Standard* of her marriage to Lawrence G. Focht of Red Oak, Iowa, in a quiet wedding at the family home at the corner of Third and Locust streets.

All was not well, however, as a week later, Isabel filed for an annulment of the marriage, claiming that her consent was obtained by threats, intimidation and fraud. The complaint stated that her parents threatened to disown her if she did not marry Mr. Focht, who had by this time left for Salt Lake City.

By August 19, the proceedings of the district court were dominated by the Focht divorce case, which was undefended, as apparently the defendant was as anxious for dissolution of the marriage as the plaintiff; the case caused quite a sensation in town, and the proceedings were watched with much interest.

Mr. Tracy testified that at the time of the marriage his daughter was in an exceedingly nervous condition, and was not accountable for what she did. He also stated that Mrs. Tracy had threatened her daughter in various ways, and told her that she would disown her if she did not submit to have the marriage ceremony performed. In the afternoon, Mrs. Tracy took the stand and testified that her daughter had always been an obedient girl, and that she had since regretted having influenced her so strongly to marry Mr. Focht.

The next day, Judge Brantly, after studying the case, refused to grant an annulment. Until her husband were to give her some grounds for divorce, she could not free herself from the obligation which she had assumed, or as the headline in the Anaconda News column of the Standard announced, 'Mrs. Isabel Focht Was Legally Matrimonified.'

Poor Isabel. She tried again in September, and again Judge Brantly refused to give an annulment, as he felt grounds were insufficient. The 1899 Anaconda City directory lists Mrs. Isabel Tracy at 320 W. Third. Inquiry with the helpful clerks of the court at Anaconda-Deer Lodge county courthouse in 1995 revealed that in the District Court of Louisa County, Iowa, in August 1899, Lawrence G. Focht was granted a divorce from Isabel Focht on the grounds of desertion, with her name restored to Tracy.

In September of that year, she was married in Butte to Watson Gaily, an employee in the General Office of the A.C.M., and they lived quietly in Anaconda at 510 Main street for 42 years, active in many church, fraternal and civic affairs.

Anne Douglas

Prior to being appointed as Miss Tracy's assistant in 1898, Anne Douglas had been a teacher at Anaconda High School. Her sojourn at the library was brief, and the Anaconda News column of January 8, 1899, announced her forthcoming marriage. 'The wedding of Miss Anne Douglas to Hiram Wease Hixon removes from Anaconda's society circles an accomplished and beautiful young lady who is widely known and a decided favorite, one whose loss will be greatly felt,' the reporter tells us, and goes on to say that Mr. Hixon was formerly connected with the Anaconda Copper Mining Company as a superintendent, but had recently made a tour of the world from which he had returned with plans to make his home in Helena.

The wedding was held at the home of the bride's mother at 714 Hickory, with W. A. Heywood as groomsman and Virginia Douglas, sister of the bride as maid of honor. Miss Norma Robinson of Deer Lodge and Miss Laura Durston of Anaconda were bridesmaids, and the ceremony was performed by Rev. E.G. Trout of Deer Lodge. After a wedding breakfast following the noon ceremony, the couple departed on the afternoon train for California where they planned to remain for a month before returning to Helena to make their home. Hiram Hixon was listed in the Helena 1898 city directory as superintendent of ASARCO, but there is no further listing for them in the Helena directories.

ANNE WHITLEY AND NELLY LATHAM

Anne Whitley of California was appointed by Mrs. Hearst in October of 1898 to fill the next vacancy at the library, so she replaced Miss Douglas for a few months and then stepped into the head librarian's position. She served in that capacity until August 19, 1900 at which time she resigned the position and returned to California.

Miss Latham worked for a few months before her marriage to Dr. Snyder, and in 1901, Elizabeth Thomson was appointed head librarian, assisted by J. Robert Emmons.

J. ROBERT EMMONS

Robert Emmons was appointed assistant by Fred Clark in 1901 and served in that capacity until 1904.

The Emmons family had settled in the Deer Lodge valley prior to the platting of the city of Anaconda. Robert's father, as had so many of the people in this story, originally been drawn from Missouri to California by the gold rush. He left California in 1881 with three other families and came by wagon team to the Deer Lodge valley. Mr. Emmons had six Clydesdale horses to pull his wagon, and he hoped to raise fine draft horses in the valley, but when the smelter was built, the smoke and fumes killed his horses.

Bob was one of ten children. His brother Sam also worked at the library in the capacity of janitor for a short time, he later served as a patrol officer for the city of Anaconda before both he and Robert went to work for the Anaconda Copper Mining Company, Robert as an engineer at the Old Works and Sam as a driver for the Copper City Commercial Company.

Elizabeth Thomson

Appointed head librarian by Fred Clark on April 26, 1901, Elizabeth L. Thomson was born at Pittsfield, Illinois, and upon arriving in Montana as a young woman, taught school at Deer Lodge for several years before moving to Anaconda to teach. She served several terms as county superintendent of schools, prior to the division of Deer Lodge and Powell counties. Miss Thomson filled the vacancy caused by the resignation of Mrs. Snyder, nee Latham, who had succeeded Anne Whitley.

Her appointment was confirmed by the first board of trustees in 1904, along with Miss Livingstone and Mr. Fee.

Miss Thomson was very capable in her capacity as librarian, and she served as president of the fledgling Montana Library Association in 1910. (The association was 5 years old at that time.)

An undated article from the Western Resources, found in Matt Kelly's scrapbook, heralds Miss Thomson as 'a person who has devoted her life to her noble calling, and one who is imbued with a genuine love for the teaching art. Certainly a most fitting choice was made when this cultured and refined lady was chosen for the post of librarian, and she is unremitting in her effort to make the library the greatest possible benefit to our people.' Miss Thomson was well read herself, and maintained the library at a high standard.

In 1905, after a trip to Milwaukee and Madison, Wisconsin, Miss Thomson recommended the board should investigate the open shelf system which was being used successfully there. She felt the plan was superior to that used in Anaconda and other Montana libraries. The board invited Henry A. Lagier, secretary of the Wisconsin free system to visit Anaconda and explain it to them. He was very impressed with Anaconda's handsome facility. Subsequently Miss Ono Mary Imhoff of Madison, was engaged at a salary of $100 per month to recatalog the library to prepare the collection for the changeover to an open shelf system.

"It is an innovation, but not an experiment that we have adopted," said board chairman, E.P. Mathewson, when the change in the system was announced. The changeover was completed in 1906.

Shortly thereafter, Miss Thomson reported the results of the first inventory to be taken, a task which required three months time. It was discovered that two books had been taken from the adult department; *The Compleat Angler,* valued at 30 cents, and *Haswell's Engineers Handbook* valued at $4.50. One 'unattractive looking book' entitled *Heart of Oak, vol.1,* was missing from the children's section and Miss Thomson fancied 'that some very young child, innocent of any wrong intention, carried it off.'

As early as 1904 Miss Thomson had mentioned to Mrs. Hearst in a letter that her health was frail and she might stay in Anaconda only for six months or a year more, although she expected the board to allow her to stay in the position as long as she wished. Ill health did finally force her retirement, but not until 1922, after nine months of illness did she finally give in. She was active in the social life not only of Anaconda, but also of Deer Lodge and Philipsburg where she had many friends. She died on May 22, 1923 at the home of her sister, Mrs. Thomas C. Irwin, in Philipsburg, and was buried at Hill Crest cemetery in Deer Lodge. The library was closed on the day of her funeral which was attended by a large number of Anacondans, including the staff of the library, Florence Catlin, Ruby Mahan and John Ahern.

Martha Livingstone

When Bob Emmons resigned as Miss Thomson's assistant in 1904, he was replaced by Martha Livingstone, who continued in that position until 1917.

Miss Livingstone was listed in the 1896 city directory as a teacher at Anaconda High School, and in the 1898 directory as the principal at the High School. She served quietly in the capacity of assistant at the library until in 1917 the board minutes record the approval of purchase of two sets of books from the private collection of Miss Livingstone, and shortly thereafter she left Anaconda to accept the position of head librarian at Lead, South Dakota.

A newspaper article from the *Lead Daily Call* for April 10, 1921, picked up by the *Anaconda Standard*, tells of a 'delightful program staged at the Hearst Library at Lead under the direction of Librarian Martha Livingstone.' The only picture of a librarian in the files of the Hearst Free Library in Anaconda is apparently Miss Livingstone, as 'Lead, South Dakota' is printed on the back of the photo.

Peggy Dobbs, librarian at the Phoebe Hearst Memorial library at Lead was unable to provide any information as to how long Miss Livingstone remained in her position there, or what became of her afterwards.

FLORENCE CATLIN

One can imagine that during Edwin B. Catlin's early tenure on the board of directors, a lot of library activity might have been discussed around the dinner table in the Catlin home. It doesn't seem too unusual that his daughter Florence would be quite interested in library affairs, and in 1918 she was hired as assistant at the library upon the departure of Martha Livingstone.

Florence was born in Syracuse, New York and arrived in Anaconda with her parents in 1889 when her father came to help establish the *Anaconda Standard* for Marcus Daly. She attended Anaconda schools and went on to graduate from the University of Montana in 1910. While at the University she was active in student affairs, especially including the Y.W.C.A. in which she held the office of vice president, and Kappa Alpha Theta sorority.

After graduation from the University, Miss Catlin returned to Anaconda, and took a position as teacher at the Lincoln school. She applied for the position of assistant librarian when Miss Livingstone resigned, and her application, after statements from Mr. Dwyer and Mr. Kennedy as to her fitness for the position, was unanimously accepted by the board of trustees.

It was the beginning of a 40 year career at the library. She assisted Miss Thomson very capably, taking virtually complete responsibility during Miss Thomson's long illness at the end of her career, and then was appointed head librarian in 1922.

Children's Book Week, which was invented by the American Booksellers Association and Associated Publishers, promoted by the American Library Association and Boy Scouts, was first observed in Anaconda in 1922 under the leadership of Florence Catlin. The children's department had been closed for a short time so inventory could be taken and books repaired, and Children's Book Week was promoted in November as a way to get parents and children into the library to discover the delights of reading. The theme was 'More Books for the Home.'

In January 1928, Mr. Rice, principal of the high school, implied that students did not seem to be welcome in the library. Miss Catlin replied that she was always willing to enable students to enjoy the benefits of the library, but that students did not always come to study, nor did they always behave properly. The board instructed her to notify Mr. Rice that students entering the library during school hours should have written permission from their teacher.

Miss Catlin was an efficient and meticulous administrator and never lost sight of the vision that Mrs. Hearst had for her gift to the people of Anaconda. Three generations of Anacondans immediately associate the memory of Miss Catlin with their fond recollections of the Hearst Free Library.

Rubietta Mahan

Miss Catlin had five different assistants during her 35 years as head librarian, The first of these was Rubietta Mahan who served for 4 years, from 1922 to 1926.

It was noted in the board minutes of September 27, 1921 that Miss Ruby Mahan, Miss Mary McCarthy and Miss May Bell

Yelman would enter the library as apprentices without pay. Then on September 26, 1922, the minutes inform us that Miss Rubietta Mahan, 'who has served as substitute for 10 months, and has recently completed 7 weeks of special training in library work at the Colorado Agricultural College, was appointed Assistant Librarian for $100 per month.'

She continued in that capacity until her resignation on February 16, 1926, when board member Rosealba Laist and Miss Catlin considered applications of possible successors to Miss Mahan, and recommended the hiring of Miss Nora M. Bentley, a college graduate with some library experience.

Nora Bentley

Nora was an Anaconda native, attending Anaconda schools and Broadway High School in Seattle. Her parents were Mr. and Mrs. Harry N. Bentley, early-day Anaconda residents. After graduation from the University of Washington in 1925, she returned to Anaconda and accepted the position at the library. She worked with Miss Catlin until shortly after her marriage to Theodore Fulmor in December of 1929.

Elizabeth Ainslie

The Ainslie family lived at 214 Elm when Elizabeth was appointed by the board of trustees to replace Nora Bentley Fulmor as assistant in early 1930. An attractive, enthusiastic young woman, Liz was active in the social life of the community. In 1935 she married Abner 'Bud' Neal from Philipsburg, and they moved to Arizona, where he worked for one of the copper companies. After Bud's death, she married her daughter-in-law's widowed father, and they continued to live in Arizona until her death in 1995. When she left the Anaconda library in 1935, the board of trustees appointed Katherine Eamon to replace her as assistant to Florence Catlin.

Katherine Eamon

A daughter of Angus J. Eamon and Mary A. Kane Eamon, Katherine was born in Anaconda and graduated from Anaconda High School in May of 1930. She went on to the University of Montana and graduated from that institution in 1934 with a

B.A. in Classical Languages. She worked at the library until she married C. M. Olsen of Missoula in June of 1936.

Mr. Olsen was employed as a Civil Engineer on government projects at Glasgow, Montana, and later at Aransas Pass, Texas. They had 3 children, two boys and a girl. Katherine was serving on a jury when she suffered a fatal heart attack in February 1971. Angus Eamon, her father, served many terms as city councilman in Anaconda, and was the first councilman appointed to represent that body on the library board of trustees.

A student in a library course at the High School, Natalie Sliepcevich, had taken training at the library and substituted for Miss Eamon upon occasion, and when Katherine submitted her resignation, the board appointed Natalie to the position of Assistant.

Natalie Sliepcevich

As with Florence Catlin, Natalie Sliepcevich's arrival at the Hearst Free Library was the beginning of a long and illustrious career.

Her parents were Maxim and Jovanka Sliepcevich, who came from Hercegovina in Yugoslavia in 1908. Her father, Max, worked at the smelter for 47 years.

During the years that she was assistant to Miss Catlin, Natalie was active in the community, particularly the Anaconda Ski Club, in which she not only was an avid skier, but also served as club secretary, and was instigator of a good many merry social events at the club house at Wraith Hill. She was a Girl Scout leader for an Anaconda troop and often recalled participating with them during World War Two in the numerous scrap drives that were conducted throughout the nation to provide necessary materials for the war effort.

Her enthusiastic touch was much in evidence at the library, with her special displays, scrapbooks and a regularly published newsletter.

Upon Miss Catlin's retirement in March of 1957, Natalie stepped easily into the position of head librarian, and the board called upon former assistant Nora Fulmor to be her assistant.

Natalie held membership in several professional organizations, including the American Library Association, the Pacific Northwest Library Association, and the Montana Library Association. Attendance at their annual conferences and numerous seminars and workshops gave her the opportunity to travel many times across the country; to San Francisco, to Chicago, to New York and Houston, each one broadening her expertise and her enthusiasm for library service. Well thought of in state library circles, she served as president of the Montana Library Association in 1963-64, and in April 1965, chaired the state conference which was held in Anaconda. State Librarian Ruth Longworth often called on Natalie to accompany her on visits to other libraries around the state.

It was during a visit east to an ALA conference in 1965 that Natalie first called on William Randolph Hearst, Jr., grandson of George and Phoebe, to acquaint him with the library and some of the problems being faced at that time. He immediately brought the matter to the attention of the Hearst Foundation resulting in a check for $6500 for urgently needed wiring and a new lighting system.

A few years later, upon hearing that Mr. Hearst was planning to be in South Dakota to dedicate U.S. Route 385, newly designated as the George and Phoebe Hearst Memorial Highway, Natalie called him again, and suggested that while he was in the area he should visit the Anaconda library. He accepted the invitation, and on July 25, 1969, Mr. Hearst and his son Austin were the honored guests at a reception at the Library. They toured the facility from top to bottom, and visited with the townspeople who have appreciated for so many years the magnificent gift of his grandmother to the people of Anaconda. Another generous check from the Hearst Foundation resulted in a cement floor in the basement and a roomy new charge desk.

"Austie and I enjoyed our trip more than I've got room to tell you," Mr. Hearst wrote to Natalie. "For me, the high point and, of course, the main reason for going, was to see the Hearst Library in Anaconda and visit with you. You were the cause— the other things were results. Really, Natalie, I don't know when I've had a busier few days or more productive or more all-around interesting and entertaining time" His letter concluded with an invitation to visit him and Mrs. Hearst in New York "to take in some real good shows." Unfortunately, she never had the opportunity to take him up on his offer.

Another check was received in 1982 which was used for much needed maintenance work, and one in 1985 provided new venetian shades throughout the building, a larger card catalog, a replacement for the worn-out photocopy machine, and a most welcomed microfilm reader-printer.

At the annual conference of the Montana Library Association held in Butte in April of 1987, Natalie was recognized by the master of ceremonies and presented with a bouquet of flowers sent by Anaconda-Deer Lodge county in appreciation of fifty years of dedicated service to the library.

Natalie retired as head librarian in December of 1987, and shortly thereafter, she left Anaconda and moved to Norman, Oklahoma were she has a home on the golf course and continues her busy and active life near her sister Elena and brother Cedomir.

Nora (Bentley) Fulmor

Natalie was assisted at the library for seven years by Nora Fulmor, who had worked as assistant to Miss Catlin until her marriage to Ted Fulmor in 1929. Mr. Fulmor was a research engineer with the Anaconda Company, and his work took them to interesting assignments in other countries. They were active in the community, being charter members of the Anaconda Ski Club, prominent in the Country Club and the Episcopal church. Nora was also busy with WAIME, the Republican Women, served as director of the Girl Scouts, and president of Chapter T of PEO. Along with all this, she raised three daughters, Phyllis, Maureen and Marjorie.

It was when the girls were raised that Nora went back to work at the library as assistant to Natalie in 1957, and she stayed until 1964, at which time she retired to spend more time with her husband. Unfortunately, Ted died in 1965 from injuries suffered in a plane crash in Salt Lake City, as he was returning from a company project in South America. Nora passed away in August of 1979 in Anaconda.

Marian Geil

When Nora retired, the application of Marian Geil was accepted by the board. A native of Anaconda, and a graduate of the University of Montana, Marian was Secretary-Manager of the Chamber of Commerce at the time, and upon leaving the staff of the chamber, she was elected to their board of directors, and subsequently moved into positions of second vice president, first vice president, and finally serviced as the first woman president of that organization in 1971. Also active in the Anaconda Ski Club, Soroptimist International, and Copper Village Museum and Arts Center, Marian's enthusiasm for research was useful in achieving National Historic Site designation for the library in 1973. She was invited to the Governor's Conference on Libraries in Helena, and took part in numerous continuing education workshops conducted by the Montana Library Association, of which she was a member.

After Natalie's retirement, Marian continued to serve as assistant until her own retirement in 1995 after 31 years of service in the library.

Julianne Shepard

The position of head librarian vacated by Natalie Sliepcevich in 1987 was given by the board to Julianne Shepard of Butte. Mrs. Shepard had a master's degree in library science from the University of Wisconsin-Milwaukee, and was the wife of the librarian at Butte Public Library. She was a member of the American and Montana Library associations, and chaired the MLA annual conference in Butte in 1987.

The hiring of an out-of-town person to head a Deer Lodge

county department created quite an uproar in town for a few months, but Juli worked well with the board and many changes were made in library policy in the 11 months she filled the position. She resigned in February 1989 as her husband had accepted a position in Tacoma, Washington.

Deni Donich Corrigan

The board advertised again for a librarian with a masters degree, and was able to fill the position with a person with Anaconda roots. In March 1989 Deni Donich Corrigan was hired as head librarian. The daughter of a former Anaconda doctor, George Donich, Deni had a masters degree in library science from Brigham Young University. She had earned her bachelors degree from Gonzaga in English Literature, and brought 10 years of experience in libraries in Utah and Montana with her. During her six years as head librarian she created an enthusiasm for reading among the younger patrons with imaginative and innovative summer reading programs which increased in participation as the years went on. Forced to retire because of ill health, Deni was replaced in January of 1996 by Honore Bray.

Honore Bray

Mrs. Bray grew up in Anaconda, the daughter of Joseph J. and Marian Lorello. After graduating from Central High School, she earned a degree in family and consumer science at Montana State University, and obtained a fifth year degree in library science. She spent 18 years at Jordan High school teaching home economics and helping out at the school library. Her expertise with computers was put to immediate use when she stepped into the position, with the acquisition once again of computers for the use of the public within the library, as well as the library's own increasing use of the computer for interlibrary loans and research projects.

Increasing community involvement in the library was her avowed goal, and her first summer reading program geared at involving families, not just children, in the activities, showed enthusiasm and good planning.

COLLEEN FEGUSON

Coming on board as Assistant to Mrs. Bray in January of 1996 was Colleen Feguson, another Anaconda native, who had been working part-time at the library for 6 years, and so was well-versed in procedures and the day by day functioning of both adult and juvenile departments of the library.

From a library oriented family, Colleen fit very easily and naturally into the position. Her father, Terry Caulfield, was librarian for many years at the Junior High School, and her sister Theresa was also a school librarian. Coincidentally, her brother-in-law Terry Ferguson was librarian at the state hospital in Warm Springs.

Her willingness to embrace the new technology and face the challenge of electronic information retrieval made Colleen a vital part of the new look at Hearst Free Library, as the Internet and Worldwide Web became part of the everyday activity of this 100 year old institution.

SUBSTITUTES

Of vital importance to the smooth functioning of the library through the years have been the substitutes—on call, usually on short notice, to step in and take care of things in the absence of the librarian or assistant.

Edith Demond	1919-1920	Betty Tuss	1984-1994
Olga McConnell	1958-1961	Nancy Bailey	1987
Kathryn Sargent	1959	Deni Corrigan	1988
Lola Kettner	1959-1980	Colleen Ferguson	1988-1996
Anne Roberts	1961	Cindy Vermiere	1994-1996
Clara Astle	1968-1980	Mary Van Slyke	1996
Eileen Murphy	1974-1980	Laurie Pecukonis	1996-
Trena Vollmer	1980-1987	Rose Mogren	1996-
Miriam Caton	1981	Susan Costle	1997-

13 The Custodians

John Fee, who was the janitor of the library when it opened in 1898, was reaffirmed to that position by the first board of trustees when they took over the responsibility for the building in 1904. Prior to his appointment to the library job, he had worked in construction for the Twohy Brothers, and then as janitor at the Lincoln school.

Early in December of 1898, just a few months after the opening of the new library, police officer Thomas Lebeouf, patrolling his regular Main street beat, was hailed by janitor John Fee, who reported he believed there were burglars in the library. Asleep in his room in the basement, Mr. Fee was awakened by men's voices and the tramp of feet above his head. The two entered the building and turned on the lights. After a thorough search, they could discover nothing amiss, but found one of the small east-side windows open about six inches. Since two attempts had been made to enter the old building, it was agreed that possibly somebody had been prowling about, but the reporter who wrote the news item for the *Anaconda Standard* could not imagine why burglars would bother to enter a library where there was very little money on hand, and if a person wanted a book, they could borrow it free in the daytime. The Standard went on to report that burglaries and attempted burglaries had been rather few and far between in Anaconda during the preceding six months.

During the final few years of his stay in Anaconda, Mr. Fee's eyes gave him increasing trouble. He finally moved to Canada to be near a brother, and while there, went totally blind. He lived in a sanitarium in Toronto for about 13 years. He corresponded regularly with friends in Anaconda, dictating his letters, and Miss Thomson reported hearing from him that E.P. Mathewson and his son Edward had called upon Mr. Fee on several occa-

John Fee, tending lilacs, 1904

sions and had given him a great treat by catching him up on Anaconda news. His brother Thomas took him into his home when a general decline in his health finally resulted in pneumonia, and he passed away soon after, on March 10. l917. He was 61 years old, and was buried in New Market, Ontario.

The record for longevity among the library's custodian-engineers goes to John Ahern, who served in that capacity for 30 years, from 1906 to 1936. He was the first of the CPE janitors, that is, his wages were the first to equal or exceed those of the head librarian, with his raise in 1907. To Mr. Ahern fell the responsibility for the 57 trees from Mr. Greig planted on the library boulevards, and the 25 yellow pine trees from Mr. Call in 1909.

Mr. Ahern helped with the book drive for the army camps during the first world war, and was in charge of the library on Sundays when the building was available for patrons to read the newspapers and do research, but no books were circulated. Obviously he could handle that duty also, as he substituted for Miss Catlin for vacation in 1925, and again in 1930, when he was paid an extra $3.00 per day in addition to his regular wages for serving in the capacity of substitute librarian.

The row with the city council over the installation of the new stoker for the library in 1932, compounded by the fact that the library board did not cut Mr. Ahern's wages when the city's janitor at city hall had to take a cut, precipitated a showdown that year. The council, in a show of force, (as warned about by Mayor Frinke in 1903,) disallowed Mr. Ahern's 14 days of paid vacation and forced him to pay back to the city the $56 that had been paid to his substitute.

By 1935, he was having trouble clearing the sidewalks of snow in the winter time, and there was talk of removing the poplar trees whose roots were raising the sidewalks. They were removed in April 1936.

Mr. Ahern was injured in a fall on November 18, and Leonard Denton, who had been substituting for him, was asked to take his place.

The next five gentlemen held the job for from one to five years. Leonard Denton was replaced in 1938 because the city council wanted an ex-serviceman in the position, and they questioned Mr. Denton's proof of citizenship. John Monahan was chosen from 13 applications. He resigned in 1942 and was replaced by Barney McTigue. McTigue died suddenly, at work, in March 1943, and was replaced by Thomas F. Murphy, who stayed until 1948. When he resigned, the position was filled by James D'Arcy, who worked until the spring of 1951, at which time John E. Walsh stepped into the position, and held it for 11 years. He was replaced briefly by Albert White, who died suddenly after just a few months on the job, and William Pilon, who had been substituting, was asked to take over.

It was during the sojourn of Bill Pilon that several book salesmen started bringing their wives through Anaconda on their vacations, to see the library. "It is absolutely the cleanest library I've ever seen!" one of them confided to the librarian. It was truly a showplace during those years. Mr. Pilon ran a shoe repair shop on Park street, and still managed to put in 8 hours at the library every day, spending most evenings during the summer hand-watering the yard. He kept the lilacs trimmed to perfection, and was responsible for the patches of lily-of-the-

Bill Pilon, 1969

valley and snow-on-the-mountains still tucked into the corners. One year he planted spruce trees on either side of the Main street door. One of them did not survive, but the other grew clear up to the drain on the roof and finally had be be removed in 1996.

If the librarian needed a different furniture arrangement to take care of the growing book collection, or improved seating arrangement for patrons, or a space for new equipment, she would pose the question of 'how to' to Mr. Pilon. He would think about it for a couple of days, and then announce, "I've got an idea!" The next day the change had been completed by the time the rest of the staff reported for work. He was innovative, enthusiastic, and took great pride in his work. He was on hand for Mr. Hearst's visit in 1969, and was a member of the Phoebe Apperson Hearst Historical Society, whose newsletter carried a notice of his death in 1974. His passing on September 5, at age 64, due to cancer, was a huge loss to the library.

Buzzy Peterson, 1976

'Buzzy' Peterson's interest in the library began the day he stepped into Mr. Pilon's shoes in 1974. He carried on the work for four years until the closure of the old city hall caused the loss of the engineer's position there, and Louis Menicucci was moved into the library position. Buzzy moved up to the court house, and soon, on top of his engineer's job, he was the city building inspector and the civil defense director. His concern for and interest in the library continued throughout and after his court house years.

When Louis Menicucci stepped into the library job, he was given a CETA employee to help out. The Comprehensive Employment and Training Act was a government program which provided federal money to municipalities for job training and public service jobs for the unemployed. Little did Kurt

The Custodians

Kurt Wyant, 1992

Wyant realize his involvement in the library under the program would turn into a career with Anaconda-Deer Lodge county. Menicucci was a good mentor for Kurt, teaching him much about carpentry and building, which stood him in good stead during the library years and later on.

Kurt's earliest acquaintance with the library came as a second grader at St. Peter's school, when the whole class went to the library every Tuesday with their teacher, Sister Theresa. At the end of the school year, the class was instructed to write an illustrated report on the various countries of the world they had studied in class. Kurt and three classmates decided the most logical way to illustrate such a paper was to cut the pictures out of the books they had read; which they did. Kurt could laugh about it many years later, but the memory made him wince. "Our parents had to pay for the books we destroyed," he recalled. It had certainly been no laughing matter to four chastened second graders.

Upon occasion, it was very useful having an athletic young man on the staff of the library. Kurt was working on the steps on the Main street entrance one day, when a young man slipped out of the building that way. The librarian stuck her head out the door and asked, "Did that fellow have a yellow book in his hand when he left?" "He sure did," Wyant replied. "Then he just stole the Chilton's Auto Repair Manual," she told him. Kurt took off like a shot. When the thief heard the rapidly closing footsteps behind him, he took off running and threw the book into a snowbank half a block up the street. Kurt retrieved it, and with a little drying off and time under the book press, it was soon back in service. The thief ended up in justice court.

One year when it was time for the Montana Library Association's annual meeting, both librarians wanted to attend, but only one substitute was available. Kurt was there anyway, so he was drafted to fill in a couple shifts. He finished his cleaning chores in the morning, popped home and put on his suit, and was behind the desk at 10 a.m. ready to check books out. The following year, one of the exhibitors at the conference asked the librarians if Kurt was still at the library. "Oh, do you know Kurt?" they asked in surprise. "I've never met him," the exhibitor laughed, but I remember last year you told us he was running the library for you so you could both come to the meeting!"

Kurt passed his engineer's test and was ready to step into the full-time position as custodian-engineer when Louie Menicucci had to retire because of ill health in 1981.

Before too long, the county took Kurt away from the library and he became full-time engineer at the court house. As his responsibilities there grew, he had less and less time to spend at the library, and in 1995, Squeaky Clean Janitorial Services was hired to do the daily cleaning. Kurt's duties spread out to cover not only maintenance at the court house and the library, but also supervision of the waste water treatment plant and a host of other duties.

He still admits to having a special affection for the institution, as does his predecessor, Buzzy Peterson. In 1995 Peterson accepted appointment to the board of trustees, and was immediately thrust into the unenviable task of making the decision to alter the building of which he and Kurt were both so proud, to make it readily accessible for handicapped patrons.

14 Reminiscences and Snappy Research Questions

In recent years, high school class reunions have become very popular, and there are usually several reunions held in town during the summer months. Many of the participants make it a point to stop in the library for a visit. The first reaction, at least before the ADA changes, was often, "This place hasn't changed in 50 years!"

One young man who returned to his 10th reunion shortly after Urban Renewal had demolished the 300 block on Park street, and the top had been taken off the Montana Hotel, looked around the library practically with tears in his eyes. "This is the first thing I've seen that's like coming home," he said quietly.

Some good stories occasionally came out of these visits. One 50 year reunion attender confided gleefully to the librarian that he recalled, as a youth, "sneaking upstairs when the librarian wasn't looking and stabbing that stuffed lion with a spear until his insides ran out!" "Yes, I know," she retorted, you're probably one of the reasons the upstairs had to be closed to the public!"

Another 'old kid' remembered moaning and howling into the outside ventilators and 'driving the librarian crazy,' possibly explaining why those vents were sealed off so many years ago.

An older woman in town for a reunion startled several patrons of the reading room by calling out loudly from the Main street door to the librarian, "Is that obscene statue still upstairs?"

An amusing story concerning the Laocoon statue came to light in 1994 when a retired gentleman who had just moved in to Hearthstone next door after living many years in California came to the library for an application for a card. He recalled applying for his first library card at this very library 70 years ago from Miss Catlin. He used to study upstairs, he said, and upon one occasion, a friend named Beatty discovered the forearm of Laocoon could be loosened, so he removed it and stuck it up his sleeve. Upon leaving the study area he walked up to Miss Catlin to thank her for letting him study upstairs, and putting out his hand to shake hands, walked away leaving the startled lady holding Laocoon's arm.

Another visitor to the library in October of 1993 recalled having spent lots of time upstairs looking at stereoscope pictures while attending Daly school. He had a little more far-fetched story to share when he asked about the statue. He had done a lot of research on it, he claimed, and it was a famous piece that Marcus Daly had bought in Europe and it sailed around the Horn before getting here to be placed in the library!

A young man came in as a teacher's assistant with Head Start group one day, and obviously enjoyed looking around. "This place doesn't change much, does it?" he confided to the librarian. He recalled that when he was a little fellow, a new sidewalk was being laid on the Fourth street entrance, and he and a young friend very cleverly wrote their names in the fresh cement. Fortunately the custodian found it before the cement dried, and was able to cover it up. "Boy, was I in trouble!" he said. "They called my dad, and I had to rake leaves around the library for a month. We were scared to death of that guy, you know, but he was really nice." The librarian agreed that Mr. Pilon took great pride in caring for the library. "Did you ever write your name on another sidewalk?" she asked. "Never wrote it again anyplace I wasn't supposed to, I really learned my lesson," he replied.

One of the assistants had a favorite story about one of the board members. When the budget was particularly tight, it was sometimes a bit of a wait before a popular title was finally in place on the shelf, and one of these titles fell into the hands of one of the trustees. She toted it home gleefully, in anticipation of a good read. Two days later, she telephone the library in a panic and spoke to the assistant. "I'm in terrible trouble!" she said. "I was sitting on the porch reading '___ __ ___ ____ ____' and my husband was watering the yard. I put the book down on the porch and went in the house to get something, and while I was inside he moved the hose. When I came back out, the water was spraying all over the book! I tried to dry it off, but it is completely destroyed! (The librarian) will just kill me, we've waited so long for that book, I know lots of people are still anxious to read it. I'll be glad to replace it," she said, "but what I want to know is, could you possibly process it and put it in circulation without (the librarian) knowing what I've done? She'll just kill me!"

The assistant assured her the job could be carried out, and sure enough, a few days later the new book was surreptitiously delivered to the library, quietly processed, and has been circulating cheerfully for several years, with nobody the wiser to its traumatic early experience.

Favorite reference questions are always a subject of great hilarity when librarians get together. It is sometimes very difficult to get a patron to tell you exactly what it is he wants to know. For example, not too long ago, a patron entered the Hearst Free Library and asked for a book on 'females.' "That's a pretty broad subject," the librarian said, groping for some way to get the lady to be more specific. "Do you mean females, as opposed to males, for instance in the job market, competing for the same job?"

"No! Not at all!" the lady replied. "You know, little females!" The librarian tried again. "Oh, you mean a book about explaining the facts of life to a young girl?" The patron gave her a withering look. "No, that's not what I want. Somebody gave me a little female dog, and I want to find a name for it." With relief, the book lady was able to hand her a copy of 'Pet Names,' certainly a far cry from the original request.

One summer evening, a young patron, probably about 12 years old at the time, marched up to the charge desk with her baseball cap on her curly head and announced, "My mother told me to get her a book. I think it's called 'Hitch of Detroit.' " "Hitch of Detroit?" the librarian was nonplussed. "That's a new one to me. Is it a new book? Did she see it on television?"

"No, I don't think so," the young lady replied. "I think she said it was a real old book, she got it here a long time ago." The librarian searched her brain frantically for any title on the shelf

119

that even remotely sounded like 'Hitch of Detroit.'

"Do you have any idea of what the book is about?" she asked her young customer. "Yes," that worthy replied, "I believe it is a book about football." This did not help the bemused librarian at all. 'Hitch of Detroit'...a story about football...an old book she had read here before...she quickly checked the card catalog under 'Football-stories' and ran her eye over the new book shelf. Nothing a parent could have requested that sounded like 'Hitch of Detroit.'

"Robin," she said finally, "You've stumped me. I just can't figure what it is your Mom wants. Do you want to telephone her and check on the title? I just can't come up with a football story called 'Hitch of Detroit' that she read here before."

The little girl went to the telephone, and carried on an animated conversation with her mother. Finally she returned to the charge desk, and announced triumphantly, "The book Mother wants me to check out for her is *The Hunchback of Notre Dame*."

One day, a usually very reliable patron called on the telephone. "I just met ___ ___ (another regular patron) on the street and she said she had just returned a wonderful book. Would you save it for me?"

"Certainly," replied the librarian, who had just come on shift. "I wasn't here when she came in, what was the name of the book?"

"I can't remember," said the caller, "but it had 'and' in it." In desperation the book dispenser looked over the cart of books waiting to be shelved, and there, fortunately, was 'Olivia and Jai' by Rebecca Ryman.

"That's it!" the caller said gleefully. "I'll pick it up later!"

"It's a good thing there wasn't time to shelve those books," the librarian thought to herself. "I'd have had a great time figuring out which book with 'and' in it was such a good read. 'North and South?' 'The Agony and the Ecstasy?' 'The Sword and the Scalpel?'

Another memorable request along that line was from a younger patron who wanted to know, "Do you have a green book behind your desk that starts with "How?"

In the interesting research question department we have recorded "Do you have a list of all the Congress and

Republicans?"

Or, "Do you have a book about the man who owns the legislature?"

A young patron in spring of 1990, confusing two of the newsworthy people of the month demanded, "Do you have a book on Noriega Mandela?"

A sixth grader came just after school started in fall of 1994 and announced, "I have to write a biography of a riddle."

"Where's the books that rhyme?" brought a smile to the face of the attendant at the charge desk one evening.

A request for a 'map of the stores' highlighted a local history project one day.

The colorful coining of words can make a regular day of questions a little more interesting in a library. One young patron announced, "I would like to know when Suzy Belle Zilch's card expands." Another wanted to know "How much does it cost to get a paper photerized?" One young lady eyed the microfilm reader when it was first installed and inquired, "Does that computer help with your arithmetic?"

The newly installed photocopy machine brought the question, "If you make a copy will it give you the piece of paper?"

Another chagrined young lady returning her overdue books and shelling out her nickels for the fine requested, "Will you wreck my card please, I don't want any more books."

One small patron who had always come in with his father, sidled up to the desk by himself one evening and inquired "Does a kid got a card named Ned Finke?" (Name changed to protect a patron now grown up.)

Library patrons are deep thinkers and sometimes share a bit of wisdom worth quoting. Former vice president Spiro T. Agnew had a novel published after he had retired from office, and although Agnew was not popular in Anaconda, several readers did check out his book with curiosity. One old timer slid it across the counter with a snort when he had finished with it and commented, "You don't have to be smart to be crooked, but you do have to be smart to write a good book."

Grandmothers are a source of wisdom too. One little fellow crept right into the fireplace one day and queried how Santa Claus could possibly see anything up there without a flashlight.

Without hesitation, his grandmother informed him that Santa did not need a flashlight because he had Rudolph!

A talkative friendly patron about age 7 discussing a book called 'Lion Cubs' which he had just chosen to check out and take home, confided in the librarian, "Lion clubs are friendly, but I wouldn't want to meet a big lion in a dark alley! Come to think of it, I wouldn't want to meet one in a sunny alley, either!"

And in conclusion to these thoughts on snappy research questions, here is the winner in that category for 1981:

High school girl: "I need a magazine for November 18, 1981."
Librarian: "What is the name of the magazine?"
Girl: "I don't know."
Librarian: "What was in it?"
Girl: "I can't remember."

Wayne Estes, Anaconda's All American as a student at Anaconda High School Circa 1961.

15 The 'Potent Factor'

One could conceivably add up all the circulation figures since 1898 and come out with a pretty good idea of how many books have been checked out from the Hearst Free library in that time, but the task is not an appealing one. Delving into those records, however, has uncovered some interesting trivia, including the months with the highest recorded circulation:

1. March 1899   7176 books
2. January 1899   6791 books
3. June 1964   6696 books

The three single days of highest recorded circulation were days that the library first re-opened after having been closed for two weeks for cleaning and varnishing the floors, and later, installing the first carpet.

1. April 22, 1913   565 books checked out
2. March 22, 1909   560 books
3. April 22, 1969   522 books

The three just plain busiest days in the library's history, without a closure to explain the desperate run on reading matter were:

1. June 3, 1963   498 books checked out
2. Sept. 8, l964   487 books
3. Sept. 7,1965   482 books

All through the 1960's, there were often days of over 400 circulation.

At any rate, Phoebe Hearst's gift to the community of Anaconda, as she predicted, has been a 'potent factor' in the lives of its people. One wonders if those Anacondans who have achieved success as authors themselves, and whose books at one time or another have graced the shelves of the library, may have received the inspiration to write those books from their early exposure to the resources of the library.

Dorothy Cooper, for example, born in Anaconda, the author of *No Little Thing*, published in 1960, receives the honor of being the author named as representing this town on the State Historical Society's Literary Map.

Probably even better remembered locally is Clyde Murphy, author of *The Glittering Hill*, a fictional rendition of the activities of the copper kings and the early days of Butte and Anaconda. Murphy is buried in Mt. Olivet cemetery.

The Cornstock Grew published in 1944, was the work of Agnes O'Neill Branscombe, wife of the local Ford dealer.

As already mentioned, Rosealba Laist's *Impressions of Europe* was a popular item among the local townspeople back in the 1930's, and a copy still survives in the archives.

Edmond 'Butch' Fahey brought the handwritten manuscript of his memoirs of bootlegging days in to the library, but neither of the staff had time to brave their way through it. Fortunately, he was determined enough to take it to the University of Montana, where it was not only read, but published under their Publications in History program, and *Rum Road to Spokane* is a valued addition to the Montana collection.

Dorothy Rochon Powers, the first woman recipient of the Ernie Pyle Memorial Award, grew up within view of the library, kitty-corner across the commons on Hickory street. She wrote for many years for the Spokesman Review, and had a book signing party in December of 1988 at the Visitor's Center for her book *Dorothy: Powers to the People,* which includes anecdotes on growing up in Anaconda. In 1960, the University of Montana presented Dorothy with the Alumni Distinguished Service Award for 'a career which has brought distinction to this University' Among her many other awards are the American Municipal Association's Award of Merit, presented in Washington, D. C. in recognition of humanitarian and meritorious service for furthering international understanding; and the National Headliners Club Award for nationwide excellence in feature writing. In the late 1950's she filled a chair in the

THE 'POTENT FACTOR'

University's School of Journalism's vaunted Dean Stone Visiting Lectures program.

Another fine author who even more recently used the facilities of the Anaconda library, (as well as many others) for his intensive research was Paul Hawkins, whose painting of the library graces the cover of this book. A versatile and multi-talented man, Paul had, at the time of his death, six manuscripts in the hands of his publisher. He brought the first copy of *The Legend of Ben Tree* into the library just a few weeks before the tragic accident that took his life.

Mike Freze, young Anaconda businessman, used his library card often in his youth. His series of religious books such as *They Bore the Wounds of Christ*, and *Making of Saints* for Sunday Visitor Publishing, have a loyal following.

Mary Paddock Berthold's fine books on Big Hole Basin history contain acknowledgements of assistance from Hearst Free library.

Matt J. Kelly and Mary Dolan, local historians used the library frequently in their research.

Patrick Morris is another author with Anaconda roots. His book, *Anaconda, Montana, Copper Smelting Boom Town on the Western Frontier*, was published in 1997. He spent many hours in the library doing research while on vacation from his home in Bethesda, Maryland.

A fine little book of poetry entitled, *A Brevity, a Brilliance and Other Poems* was authored by Virginia Hasley Brunton. She was born in Anaconda, the daughter of a mining engineer, and graduated from Anaconda High School.

No discussion of books by Anaconda authors would be complete without mentioning two popular works by artist-historian Bob Vine, *Anaconda Memories*, and *Women of the Washoe*.

The library is happy to claim as a former patron, Lester Thurow, economist and writer, whose books on the economic future of America have made the national best seller list. Lester lived with his parents and brothers, Glen and Charles, at 208 E. Third street, while his father was pastor of the First Methodist church. Lester graduated from AHS in 1956, received his B.S. from Williams College, his Masters degree from Oxford, where he was a Rhodes Scholar, and his PhD. from Harvard. He has had a distinguished career on the faculty of Massachusetts Institute of Technology. His books include *Zero-sum Society, Dangerous Currents, Zero-sum Solution, Head to Head,* and *The Future of Capitalism.*

There are many distinguished 'alumni' of the library who have gone on to make their marks in an endless variety of endeavors throughout the world, and who undoubtedly would recall the stimulus they received at their hometown library.

Lester R. Dragstedt, valedictorian of the AHS class of 1911 made an outstanding name for himself as a surgeon and physiologist His long teaching career at the University of Chicago began in 1920, and he was named Chairman of the Department of Surgery there in 1948. He was responsible for more than 360 articles published in various scientific journals, and was highly regarded for his contributions in the field of gastrointestinal physiology and important innovations in clinical surgery, particularly in the understanding and management of ulcers. He was widely sought as a lecturer and received many honorary degrees and awards. Among these he most valued his election to the National Academy of Sciences, and his award by the King of Sweden of the Order of the North Star.

Dr. Dragstedt's brother Carl A. Dragstedt was also an outstanding scientist, well known in the field of histamines, anaphylaxis and allergies. He was chairman of Northwestern University's pharmacology department. He served as chairman of the American Medical Association's experimental medicine and therapeutics section and was president of the American Society of Pharmacology and Experimental Therapeutics. He too was the author of more than 140 articles in scientific journals.

The parents of these two illustrious scientists were John A. and Caroline Dragstedt, Swedish immigrants to Anaconda, who lived at 514 Elm street, while John was a foreman of the blacksmith shop at the foundry.

A complete list of those successful people who have been influenced by the Hearst Free Library would be very impressive. Equally important are those multitudes who may not have distinguished themselves in such prominent ways, but who received the 'stimulation and influence for good' necessary to improving their lives in the manner envisioned by Phoebe

THE 'POTENT FACTOR'

Hearst in planning her magnificent gift to a humble smelter town so many years ago.

Vera Praast, homemaker, amateur writer, journalist, historian, was kind enough to write to the staff of the library upon occasion to remind them what a 'potent factor' the library had been in the lives of her family. Upon hearing of the death of Florence Catlin, Mrs. Praast, living then in Great Falls, wrote a letter to the Montana Standard, in which she stated:"For many years Miss Catlin was the librarian at the beautiful Hearst Library at Anaconda. To our family, Miss Catlin was the library; especially to our youngest son, Ted. Ted, before he entered school, had us read aloud to him. He liked Kipling's *The Cat that Walked,* and the Dr. Seuss books, particularly. Our son Bill went in for sports books; our daughter, Virginia, for poetry; my husband for Montana history, and I read mysteries, as well as what the others brought home. I have found that all librarians are kind and helpful and happy to help people enter the great world of books, which is the world of the past and the future as well as the present. Miss Catlin was especially willing. Later at the Hearst Library were other wonderful librarians, Mrs. Fulmor, Miss Sliepcevich, and Miss Geil." She concluded her letter with "Miss Catlin and her books, and her sister Mrs. Pickell with her flowers at Washoe Park, helped make our years in Anaconda happy ones that we love to think back on, and feel homesick for..."

The community of Anaconda celebrated its centennial in 1983. Of Marcus Daly's there is not much left. His home at Sixth and Hickory was razed about 1950 to make way for the gymnasium. The only remembrance of his famous racetrack are the streets of the residential area that now covers the space which bear the names of three of his favorite racers; Tammany, Hamburg, and Ogden. The Daly Bank is gone, the Montana Hotel is no more, and all that is left of the smelter is the colossal big stack, a forlorn monument to the memory of the mighty smelting works that made 'Anaconda' a name recognized around the world.

But still standing sedately on the corner of Fourth and Main streets, serenely ready to sail into its second 100 years, is the Hearst Free Library. Frank Van Trees' charming building, lovingly cared for through the century, almost made its first hundred years unchanged, until the Americans with Disabilities Act of 1992 made it imperative to alter the Main street entrance and the main reading room to provide access to the handicapped. But the graceful edifice still offers 'solace and intellectual pleasure' to the people of Anaconda.

Hopefully, the people, upon the occasion of its centennial, will recall the memory of George Hearst, whose knowledge, foresight, and fidelity in friendship, played such a crucial part in the founding of Anaconda. And hopefully, they will remember too, Phoebe Apperson Hearst, the kind and generous woman who shared his life and his fortunes and did her best to see that George would be remembered for what he was. The inscription she chose for the cornerstone on the Mining Building at the University of California reads simply,

THIS BUILDING STANDS AS A MEMORIAL TO
GEORGE HEARST—

A PLAIN HONEST MAN, AND A GOOD MINER.

Story Hour-Book Week, Carra and Becky Brolin, Vonnie Eastham. April 22, 1961

Bibliography

Bonfils, Winifred Black: *The Life and Personality of Phoebe Apperson Hearst.* Friends of Hearst Castle, San Simeon, California, 1991.

Brother Cornelius, F.S.C. *Keith: Old Master of California.* G. P. Putnam Sons, N.Y. 1942.

Davis, John F. *California, Romantic and Resourceful.* A. M. Robertson, San Francisco, California; 1914.

Fielder, Mildred. *The Treasure of Homestake Gold.* North Plains Press; Aberdeen, S.D. 1970.

Frazier, Si and Ann: *Kellogg and His Jack. Lapidary Journal;* January, 1994.

Fries, Waldemar H. *The Double Elephant Folio: The Story of Audubon's Birds of America.* American Library Association, Chicago, 1973.

Hearst, William R. Jr. *The Hearsts, Father and Son.* Roberts and Rinehart; Colorado, 1991.

Keeler, Charles. *San Francisco and Thereabout.* A. M. Robertson; San Francisco, 1906.

Laird, Helen. *Carl Oscar Borg and the Magic Region.* Gibbs M. Smith, Inc. Peregrine Smith Books; Layton, Utah, 1986.

Lead Daily Call, April 3-May 19, 1984.

Longstreth, Richard. *On the Edge of the World; Four Architects of San Francisco At the Turn of the Century.* Architectural History Foundation, N.Y. MIT Press; Cambridge, Mass. 1983.

Marcosson, Isaac F. *Anaconda.* Dodd, Mead and Co. N.Y. 1957.

Memorial Addresses on the Life and Character of George Hearst. Published by Order of Congress. Gov't Printing Office, Washington, D.C. 1894.

Miller, Lois. *Library at Lead Is Monument to Philanthropist.* Rapid City Daily Journal, Nov. 29, 1953.

Milton, John R. *South Dakota Bicentennial History.* Norton Co. 1977.

Neuhaus, Eugen. *William Keith, the Man and the Artist.* U. of Cal. Press; Berkeley, Cal. 1938.

Older, Mr. and Mrs. Fremont. *The Life of George Hearst, California Pioneer.* Printed for William Randolph Hearst by John Henry Nash, San Francisco, Cal. 1933.

Robinson, Judith. *The Hearsts: An American Dynasty.* U. of Delaware Press, 1991.

San Francisco Chronicle, May 8, 1914 (Van Trees obit.)

San Francisco Chronicle, Dec. 24, 1923 (Clark obit.)

San Francisco Examiner, Dec. 23, 1923 (Clark obit.)

Shoebotham, H. Minar. *Anaconda: Life of Marcus Daly, the Copper King.* Stackpole Company, Pennsylvania, 1956.

Acknowledgments:

Thanks to the following people for their assistance.

Donald Andreini, San Francisco Architectural Heritage; San Francisco, Cal.
Lucille Balfour, Florence, Oregon
Honore Bray, Hearst Free Library, Anaconda
Helen Brown Britton, Salt Lake City, Utah
Elizabeth Douthitt Byrne, Environmental Design Library, U. of Cal. Berkeley, H. Raphael Chacon, Ass't Prof. Art History, U. of Mont. Missoula, Montana.
Sandra Conrady, General Federation of Women's Clubs, Anaconda, Mont.
Kathleen A. Correia, California State Library, Sacramento, Cal.
Peggy Dobbs, Phoebe Apperson Hearst Library, Lead, South Dakota.
Mary Dyas, El Cajon, California
Don Eamon, Lakewood, Colorado
Colleen Ferguson, Hearst Free Library, Anaconda
Phil Geil, Anaconda, Montana
Mildred Hamilton, Special Consultant, Hearst Foundation, San Francisco, Cal.
Jerry Hansen, Anaconda-Deer Lodge Co. Historical Society; Anaconda.
Bonnie Hardwick, Bancroft Library, Berkeley, California.
John Landor, M.D. State U. of N.Y. Health Science Center at Brooklyn, N.Y.
Frances P. Lederer, Nat. Gallery of Art, Washington, D. C.
Pat Lynagh, National Museum of American Art, Washington, D. C.
JoAnne Ainslie McCroskey, Eagle, Idaho
Marjorie Marcotte, Anaconda, Montana
Pauline and Norman Marcotte, Englewood, Colorado
Erling Oelz, Mansfield Library, U. of Montana; Missoula, Montana
Theresa Orrino and staff, Court Clerk's office, Anaconda-Deer Lodge Co.
Leslie Overstreet, Nat. Museum of American History, Washington, D.C.
Laurie Pecukonis, Anaconda, Montana

Harvey Ravndahl, Anaconda Water Department, Anaconda, Mt.
Mabel Reed, Phoebe Apperson Hearst Historical Soc. St. Clair, Mo.
LaVera Rose, Manuscript Curator, S. D. Historical Archives, Pierre, S.D.
Ralph Schmidt, Anaconda Agency Photo; Anaconda, Montana
Lee Ann Schumacher, Phoebe Apperson Hearst Library, Lead, S.D.
Brian Shovers, Montana Historical Society Library; Helena, Montana
Natalie Sliepcevich, Norman, Oklahoma
Tracey Sweeney and staff, Clerk & Recorder's Office, Anaconda
Bess Vance, special assignments in San Francisco and Berkeley, Ca.
Drew Van Fossen, Managing Editor, Montana Standard, Butte, Montana.
Christopher With, National Gallery of Art, Washington, D.C.
Glenn and Pat Wallace, Bigfork, Montana
Betty Wyant, Anaconda, Montana
Terri Yeager, Hearst Foundation, San Francisco, California.

Index

Agassiz portrait, 38, 77, 88-89
Agnew, Spiro T., 121
Agricultural College, (Bozeman), 34
Ahern, John, 101, 112-113
Ainslie, Elizabeth, 104
Amalgamated Copper Co., 8
American Library Assoc., 103, 106, 129
Americans with Disabilities Act, 128, 76
Anaconda Central High School, 32
Anaconda Club, 52, 55, 57-58
Anaconda Co., (also A.C.M.), 8, 58-60, 74, 93, 98, 107
Anaconda-Deer Lodge Co., 74, 98, 107, 115
Anaconda High School, 52, 57, 63, 98, 102, 104, 122, 125
Anaconda Mine, 1, 5, 40
Anaconda, Mont., 5, 20, 25, 33, 49, 53, 56
Anaconda Recorder, 33
Anaconda Reduction Works, 5, 51
Anaconda Review, 5
Anaconda Standard, 6, 8, 10, 26-27, 29, 31, 97, 102, 111, 33, 35-36, 41, 44, 49, 51-52, 57, 61-62, 68, 70, 77
Anaconda Tin Shop, 71
Anderson, Carl, 65
annual duckfest, 55
Anthony, Miss ___, 30
Anthony, Mrs. ___, 30
Apperson, Annie, 30
Apperson, Elbert, 15, 18, 30
Apperson, Phoebe, 3, 15-16, 20-21, 76, 128
Apperson, Randolph W., 13, 15
art collection, 77, 94
ASARCO, 99
Astle, Clara, 110
Audubon, James Woodhouse, 91-92
Audubon, John James, 92
Audubon's *Birds of America*, 91

Babbitt, Charles H., 26, 28, 95
Bailey, Nancy, 110

Ballard, Bob, 66
Bancroft Library, 95, 97, 131
Bayview Racetrack, 18
Beausoleil, Paul, 66
Ben Ali (race horse), 7-8
Berthold, Mary Paddock, 125
Bien, Julius, 91
Blattner, Al, 71
'Bliss suit,' (smoke case), 53
Boardman, J. R., 43
Boone, Daniel, 15
Borein, Ed, 81
Borg, Carl Oscar, 78-79, 81, 129
Bower, W. A., 51
Branscombe, Agnes, 124
Brantly, Judge Theodore, 33, 96
Braun, Adolphe, 87-88
Bray, Honore, 109
British American Nickel Corp., 54
Broad Valleys Federation, 75-76
Brolin, Carra, 65
Brown, A. Page, 31
Brunton, Virginia Hasley, 125
Budd, Gov., (Calif.), 34
Butte, Anaconda, Pacific RR, 32
Butte Free Library, 35
Butte Water Co., 13
Byrne, Peter, 65

California gold rush, 2
Call, Mr. ___ (forester), 68, 112
Campbell, Georgina, 82
Capron, Mrs. W. C., 65
Carmichael, Ruth, 72
Carnahan, Rev. Dr., 68
Carpenters Local, 54
Catlin, Edwin B., 57, 64, 102
Catlin, Florence, 101-105, 127
Caton, Miriam, 110
Caulfield, Terry, 110
Caulfield, Theresa, 110
Centennial, library, 76
circulation statistics, 123
city common, 44, 51
City Council, 25, 34, 113
City Council (Anaconda,), 45
city reservoir, 9-11
Clark and Pearson, fence, 71
Clark, Austin, 20, 96

Clark, Edward H., 20-22, 77, 96
Clark, Fred, 20, 26, 29, 31-32, 41-42, 67, 91, 95-97, 99-100
Clark, Sen. W. A., 84
Clifford, John E. 'Jerry', 60-61, 64
Community Development Office, 73-74
Comstock Lode, 3
Comstock, William, 3
Conrady, Sandra, 66, 131
Constitutional Convention (1889), 50
Cooper, Dorothy, 124
Copper City Com'l Co., 40, 49, 100
copper production, 52
Copper Village Museum, 93, 108
Corrigan, Deni Donich, 109
Costle, Susan, 110
curling, sport, 51
Currie, Mary, 66
Curry, Larry (author), 85

Daly Bank & Trust Co., 49, 127
Daly, Donohue & Greenwood, 49
Daly, Marcus, 1, 3-5, 7-8, 56-57, 102, 118, 127, 130
D'Arcy, James, 113
Davies, ___ (Butte librarian), 26
Davis, Frances, 64, 66
Deer Lodge Co., 13, 50, 58, 61
DeLong, Naomi, 66
Demond, Charles, 64
Demond, Edith, 110
Dempsey, T. J., 29
Denny, Henry A., 47, 49, 62
Denton, Leonard, 113
Dobbins, J. W., 52
Dobbs, Peggy, 102, 131
Dolan, Mary, 76, 125
Dougherty, Elizabeth Walker, 61, 65
Douglas, Anne, 31, 96, 98-99
Douglas, Virginia, 99
Dragstedt, Carl A., 126
Dragstedt, John and Caroline, 126
Dragstedt, Lester R., 52, 126
Drescher, JoEllen, 66
Dudas, Lazlo, 93
Dumonthier, William, 65

133

Durston, J. H., 33, 57
Durston, Laura, 99
Dwyer, William K., 57-58, 65, 68, 103

Eagles Auxiliary, 74
Eamon, Angus, 65, 104-105
Eamon, Katherine, 104
Eastham, Vonnie, 72, 128
Eck, Theodore, 71
Eckstein, Ruth, 93
El Dorado, 3, 6
Eldred, L. E., 81
Elias, Alfred, 87
elk planting, 53
Elk's Club, 72
Emmons, Robert, 42, 99-101
Emmons, Sam, 100
Evans, Maggie, 4

Fahey, Edmond 'Butch', 124
Falstaff (painting), 92
Fee, John, 47, 111-112
Ferguson, Colleen, 110, 131
Ferguson, Terry, 110
Ferris, Mrs.___ (S.D.), 21
Fielder, Mildred, 8, 21
Fifer Gulch, 13
Finnegan, Frank, 65
Fire Department, 70
Fitzpatrick, Natalie, 63, 65
Flathead Lake, 52
Fleming, Raymond, 65
flood of 1938, 12-13
Focht, Lawrence, 97-98
Franklin Co., Mo., 15, 96
Frankovich, Fred, 65
Frazier, Anne and Si, 86
Freze, Mike, 125
Frinke, John W., 44-46
Fulmor, Nora Bentley, 104, 106-108, 127

Gaily, Watson, 98
Gallik, Lorraine Biggs, 66
Gates, Don, 65
Gaylord Electric Bookcharger, 71
Geil, Marian, 66, 108, 127
Gen'l Fed. Women's Clubs, 68, 131
George & Phoebe Hearst Memorial Highway, 106
Glynn, Robert, 65

Greenwood, M. B., 47, 64
Greig, Mr. ___, 68, 112
Grier, T. J., 21, 24
Gun Club, 51, 53-54

Haggin, James B., 1, 3-4, 6, 18
Hamburg, (race horse), 127
Hammerslough, Max, 55
Hammond, Harold, 65
Harvard University, 19
Hawkins, Paul A., 125
Head Start Program, 118
Hearst, Austin, 106
Hearst Corporation, 73
Hearst, Elizabeth, 4
Hearst Estate, 22, 97
Hearst Foundation, 23, 73, 75, 106, 131-132
Hearst Free Library, 26, 28, 30-31, 37-38, 40, 44-46, 64, 68-69, 77, 85, 88, 94-96, 102-103, 105, 110, 119, 123, 125-127
Hearst, George, 1-2, 4-5, 7, 15, 17, 45, 96, 128
Hearst, George, (portrait), 82
Hearst Gulch, 9
Hearst Lake, 5, 9-10, 12-13, 34
Hearst Mercantile, 21
Hearst, Millicent and boys, 73
Hearst, Mrs. Phoebe, 18, 25-27, 30, 42-45, 48, 67-68, 73, 76-80, 95, 101, 123, 126-127
Hearst, Mrs. Phoebe, (death), 69
Hearst, Mrs. Phoebe, (speech), 35-36
Hearst, William Randolph, 18, 73, 94, 130
Hearst, William R. Jr., 74, 106, 129
Hensley, Helen, 95
Herkomer, Hubert, 80-81
Heywood, W. A., 99
Hixon, Hiram Wease, 98
Homestake Gold, 21
Homestake Library, 22-23
Homestake Mine, 5, 20-24
Homestake Mining Co., 21, 24, 96
Homestake Recreation Bldg., 21
Hooe, James C., 45
horse racing, 7-8, 18
Hoyt, Maurice, 65
Hunchback of Notre Dame, 120
Hurley, Frank, 47, 49, 64

Indenture of 1904, 67

Jackass Gulch, (Cal.), 3
Jackson, George, 51, 64
Jackson, William Henry, 89
Jacques, Leo, 65
Jenny, Warren, 51, 64, 79
Johnson, Loyal, 65
Johnson, Margaret, 96
Johnson, Mary E., 61, 65
Johnson, Oscar A., 61, 65
Judith Springs, (Mo.), 2
Junior Women's Club, 76

Keith, William A., 77-78
Kellogg, Noah, 86-87
Kelly, Leo V., 65
Kelly, Matt J., 100, 125
Kennedy, Frank, 58-60, 64, 103
Keppler Jewelry, 94
Kettner, Lola, 110
Kiwanis Club, 93
Knights of Columbus, 32, 58
Kovacich, Mike, 76
Kunkel, Mrs. E. L., 65

Laist, Frederick, 55, 62
Laist, Rosealba, 62, 65, 104, 124
Lane, Agnes, 30
Laocoon and the Sea Serpents, 90-91, 117-118
Lapidary Journal, 86
Lappin, Ellen, 66
Larison, Eldon, 65
Larson, Ole, 12
Latham, Nelly, 42, 99
Law, William, 91
Lawrence County (S.D.), 23
Lead Daily Call, 24, 102
Lead, South Dakota, 20-21, 23-24, 26, 42, 96, 102
Lebeouf, Thomas, 111
Leonard, Thomas B., 65
Library 75th anniversary, 73, 83
Lick House, 18
Livingstone, Martha E., 47, 100, 101-102
Longworth, Ruth, 106
Lotus (motorboat), 52
Lotz, Mathilda, 86
Lubke, Anthony, 65

McCarthy, Mary, 103
McCarthy, Theresa, 66
McComb, Leonard, 92
McConnell, Olga, 110
McCrea, Hollis, 65
McEwan, Robert, 65
McIntyre, Dave, 65
McLean, Rose, 63, 65
McMonigle ranch, 13
McNelis, Tom, 66
McTigue, Barney, 71, 113
Mahan, Rubietta, 101, 103-104
Mahoney, Thomas F., 29, 95
Maine, (battleship), 93-94
Malcomson, Charles T., 40
Marcotte Electric, 73
Margaret Theater, 33, 52
Martin, Jack, 28, 93
Mathewson, Edward P., 47, 50-57, 62, 64, 90, 92, 101, 111
Matts, Elmer D., 34
Mee, Michael, 65
Mehrens, Wallace, 65
memorial shield, 40
Menicucci, Louis, 114
Meramec Iron Works, 16
Miller, Knute, 94
Miller, Lois, 21
Miners Union Opera House, 21
Mogren, Rose, 110
Monahan, John, 113
Montana Good Roads Congress, 52
Montana Historical Society, 36, 83
Montana Hotel, 9, 72, 117, 127
Montana Library Assoc.72, 100, 106, 108
MLA Conference, 72, 106-108
Montana Supreme Court, 35
Montgomery, W. M., 55
Morris, Patrick F., 125
Mount Haggin, 5, 7, 9
Murphy, Clyde, 124
Murphy, Eileen, 110
Murphy, Thomas F., 113

National Cathedral School, 18-19
National Register of Historic Places, 64, 73, 77
Nicely, Charles, 12

Ogden, (race horse), 127

'Old Baldy' (Mt. Haggin), 5
Old Works, 7, 92, 100
Olivia and Jai, 120
Olsen, C. M., 105
Ophir Mine, (Cal.), 3
Ophir Mine, (Utah), 4
Oreskovich, Mary Jo, 66
O'Leary, Timothy, 34
O'Shaughnessy's Saloon, 5

Palethorpe, Mary Jane, 21
Panama-Pacific Exposition, 53, 80
Park City, Utah, 4
Partington, Richard Langtry, 79, 81
Peck, Janet, 17
Peck, Mr. and Mrs. James, 17
Peck, Orrin, 18
Peckham, Richard B., 44
Pecukonis, Laurie, 110
Peterson, E. L. 'Buzzy', 66, 114, 116
Phoebe Apperson Hearst Historical Society, 114
Phoebe Apperson Hearst Library, 21, 23-24
Pilon, William, 113
Placerville, (Ca.), 3
PNLA Quarterly, 92
Powers, Dorothy Rochon, 124
Praast, Vera, 127

racetracks, 18, 127
Rancho del Poza de Varona, 31
Renaissance portrait reproductions, 93
Repath, C. H., 64
Ried's Pond, 28
Rincon Hill, 18
Roberts, Anne, 110
Robinson, Judith, 8, 20, 72
Robinson, Mrs. __., 30
Robinson, Norma, 99
rock collection, 93
Rogers, Mrs. S. S., 65
Rotary Club, 51, 55
Russell, Charles M., 54, 62
Ryan, James P., 64

San Francisco, 1, 4, 7, 17-18, 23, 30-31, 40-41, 78-80, 86-87, 90-91, 96-97, 106
San Francisco Chronicle, 73

Sargent, Kathryn, 110
Schmidt, Lianna, 66, 71
Schmidt, William, 71
Schulte, Jack, 66
Schweinfurth, Charles, 25, 31
Shepard, Julianne, 108
Siders, Debbie, 66
Silver Lake, 53
Ski Club, 105, 107-108
Sliepcevich, Cedomir and Elena, 107
Sliepcevich, Jovanka, 105
Sliepcevich, Maxim, 105
Sliepcevich, Natalie, 72-75, 105, 108
smelters, 3, 5-6, 14, 20, 34, 40, 50, 54-56, 58, 61-62, 68-69, 75, 99, 105, 127,
Smith, Frank (Helena), 52
Smith, Richard, deB., 26, 28, 95-96, 93
Smith, Robert B. (Gov.), 33
smoke case, 53
Snyder, Dr. N., 99
Socialist party, 44
Sonora, (steamship), 17
Soroptimist Club, 72
Spanish War Veterans, 93
Spanish-American War, 94
special library fund, 76
Spellman, Catherine, 76
Spraycar, William, 64, 66, 73
Squeaky Clean Janitorial Serv., 116
St. Clair, Mo., 1
State Automobile Assoc., 52
state fair, 52
State Fish Hatchery, 52
Steelville Academy, 15
Stevenson House, 18
Stevenson, Kalmar, 93
Stone, Arthur L., 61, 64, 125
stuffed animals, 68, 93
Superfund Repository, 76

Tammany, (race horse), 127
Temporary library, 25, 27, 30-32, 90, 93
Terry, John C., 52
Tevis, Lloyd, 1-2, 4-7, 18
Thomson, Elizabeth, 42, 47, 99-100
Thurow, Lester, 125

135

Toft, Peter Peterson, 86
Toole, John R., 32
Tracy, Isabel, 29, 40, 96-98
Trout, Rev. E. G., 99
Troyer, Agnes, 63, 65
Tucker, Frank, 91
Tuss, Betty, 110
Tuttle, C. A., 50, 64
Twentieth Cent. Athletic Club, 32
Twohy, James C., 31

Ungaretti, Mario, 65
United States Senate, 5, 19
U. S. Supreme Court, 53
University of California, 20, 43, 128
University of Montana, 34, 61, 102, 104, 108, 124

Van Bockern, Rev. George, 65
Van Slyke, Mary, 110
Van Trees, Frank S., 31, 40
Vermiere, Cindy, 110
Vernon, Peir, 81
Vickery, W. K., 87-88
Vine, Bob, 125
Vollmer, Trena, 110
Voorhees, James Paxton, 83

Walker Bros., 4
Wallace, Helen, 62-63, 65
Walsh, John E., 113
Walsh, Thomas J., 65
Warm Springs Creek, 5, 10, 12-13
Warm Springs Game Farm, 13
Washington, D. C., 5, 18-19
Washoe Copper Mining Co., 5
Washoe Gold and Silver Co., 5
Washoe Park, 51, 68, 127
Washoe Reduction Works, lithograph, 92
Washoe-Wasseau, 3
White, Albert, 113
White, Jack, 65
Whitley, Angela, 96
Whitley, Anne, 42, 99-100
Whitmire Settlement, Mo., 15
Winston, George B., 47, 50, 64
Winston, Mrs. George, 67, 97
Women's Club, 63, 67-72, 74, 76, 97
Women's Literary Club, 67-68, 97

World Museum of Mining, 1
World War One, 69
World War Two, 105
Wraith, William, 68
Wyant, Betty, 66
Wyant, Kurt, 115

Yelman, May Bell, 103
Yeoman, Bill, 65